To Herb and Nancy Meyer,

Yes it's true, that *is* my picture on the book jacket! This is my first attempt at writing a book. As with all first attempts this first edition is not without typos. This being an original first edition, might be worth something if I get famous some-day. It's a book that is written in the tradition of THE air force that you and I remember. I hope you both like it.

Best Wishes
Ron Moyne

P.S. TO THE COLONEL,
IT'S OKAY TO ACCEPT THIS GIFT FROM AN NCO — AFR 30-30 NO LONGER APPLIES! ☺

A Star of Honor

A Star of Honor

by

Ron Moyne

Ashley Books, Inc.
Ft. Lauderdale, FL 33319

STAR OF HONOR
Copyright © 1990 by Ron Moyne.

Library of Congress CIP Number:89-273
ISBN:0-87949-302-X

ASHLEY BOOKS, INC / Publishers
Fort Lauderdale, Florida 33319

Printed In The United States of America
First Edition

All rights reserved. No part of this book may be used or reproduced in any manner whatsoever without written permission except in the case of brief quotations in articles and reviews. Address all inquiries to ASHLEY BOOKS, INC., 4600 W. Commercial Blvd, Fort Lauderdale, Florida 33319.

Library of Congress Cataloging in Publication Data:

  Moyne, Ron, 1949-
    A star of honor / Ron Moyne.
      p.   cm.
  ISBN 0-87949-302-X
  I. Title.
  PS3563.097S74   1989   89-273
  813'.54—dc19   CIP

Dedication

This book is dedicated to all the men and women who made the ultimate sacrifice for their country. They are the veterans of the Vietnam era, the former POWs, and the brave, but not forgotten, who are still missing in action in Southeast Asia for nearly two decades. This book is also dedicated to a very special lady, Deb Prokop. Without her constant, untiring devotion and encouragement, unselfishly given to this project, this story might never have been told.

This is a work of fiction. The characters, incidents, and dialogues are products of the author's imagination and are not to be construed as real. Where the names of actual persons, living or dead, are used, the situations, incidents and dialogues concerning those persons are entirely fictional and are not intended to depict any actual events or change the entirely fictional character of the work.

The Vietnam Unknown

Where am I? Comes a puzzled sigh,
I'm hit! Reports an anguished cry.
My plane is dropping from the sky,
I fear today that I might die.

The canopy has flown astray,
It's now unto my God I pray.
Steady onward down I fall,
Hoping rescue heard my call.

My chute sways just above the ground,
And then I hear that awful sound.
A tracer bullet ends my strife,
It rips my flight suit like a knife.

I crash into the paddies low,
Will I be found? I do not know.
I love my children and my wife,
I'm just too young to end my life.

Many years have passed you see,
Has my country now forgotten me?
But through the jungles now they roam,
Have they come to take me home?

Again I fly across the sea,
One lonely passenger, that's me.
They check me out by teeth and bone,
But my records say that I'm unknown.

More years have passed in darkness gray,
Until the glory of this day.
So long I've waited this to be,
Again the light now I can see.

Awakened from my musty bed,
And placed amongst the honored dead.
I see a statue, Veterans three,
They fought and died to keep us free.

And a monument so black and bold,
I see my name! It's etched in gold!
Multitudes are in this place,
They come to share with me this grace.

A President comes to bring a wreath,
And proudly I will rest beneath.
And in the memories of all,
Of all in service who hath fall.

It's all of them I represent,
And from our country honor sent.
The people pray, the people cry,
For all the unknowns who will die.

The generations come and go,
My identity they'll never know.
For only God knows who I am,
The honored unknown, from Vietnam.

—*Ron Moyne*

Introduction

As if engulfed by an evil cloud of smoke, I am transported through a portal of time which seems never laid to rest. The reality interacts with the fantasy, and the fantasy interacts with the horrors, and the horrors remain branded upon my soul.

The raindrops, hot as glowing meteorites, never heed my pleas, and never stop tormenting my bullet-riddled body which just wants to be left alone to die in an unforgiving jungle, in an unforgiving war.

I cry out for help, but no one hears. The stench of death is foul upon the air, but I must go on. I will go on. I will never give up, and I refuse to die in this place called Vietnam, the playground of Satan himself.

Chapter 1

In a darkened hospital room he lie, a boy forced into manhood by the mistakes of another generation. His memory clouded with the evils of war; his body wrapped tightly in clean white bandages. He slowly passed the time by watching the steady drip, drip of the two bottles hanging on a stand just above his head, as they silently replaced the precious fluids of life, taken by an unforgiving jungle.

A young nurse, wearing a spotless uniform of snowy white, approached his bed. The silver bars on her collar identified her as a captain. She held his wrist and checked his pulse, as she recorded the results on a chart usually hung on a hook in front of the bed. He supposed her black hair was long, but pinned up according to regulations. Her skin was a deep copper brown, and to him, she resembled an angel. In reality, she was a Philippine National, educated in the United States, and now a nurse in the American Air Force. From a small tray, she produced a much needed injection of morphine.

"How's my favorite patient?"

A Star of Honor

"Who wants to know?" he replied sarcastically.

"You have some important visitors, today!" she announced cheerfully, as she turned him over and injected him. A quick burst of relief replaced the extreme pain and anguish.

"I don't want to see nobody, and I don't want nobody to see me!," his face red with anger.

"You have to see these people. This is your day, honey! This is your day!" She diligently gathered up her supplies, replaced the chart, and left the room to tend to other young victims. His attention again focused on the steady, seemingly never-ending drip of cold fluid entering his hand from the two, now half-empty, glass bottles.

A well-dressed man approached his bed, carrying what appeared to be two small boxes. He was accompanied by two men attired in military uniforms. Each had a row of shining stars on their shoulders, and rows of colorful ribbons adorning their chests. Many reporters ran into the room, flashbulbs popping wildly. The man was the President of the United States, and his companions were two of the highest ranking generals to command in Vietnam.

"I understand you are quite a hero, son," stated the President. "Son, you have gone above and beyond the call of duty. Your country is so very proud, and owes you a debt of gratitude."

One of the hinged boxes squeaked as he opened it. Carefully, a medal cast in the shape of a golden star with a tiny star of silver in its center was removed from the gray velvet lining it rested upon. It hung proudly from its beautiful red, white, and blue ribbon as it was pinned to his bandages. "I present you with the Silver Star, for galantry in the face of the enemy." The other box was immediately opened, and a second medal removed. Its shape was of a golden heart, with a center of purple—partially obscured by a gold silhouette of George Washington. It was hanging from a purple ribbon bordered by white stripes. The symbol of pride and honor was pinned on the airman. "I now

A Star of Honor

present you with the Purple Heart for the wounds you have sustained during this valiant action. God bless you, son." The President whispered something into his ear, and it brought a brief smile to his face. He then pointed to the door, and at that moment, the mother of the wounded airman was escorted to his bedside. She was a woman of medium height, wearing gold-rimmed, wire-framed glasses, and a multicolored dress. She carried rosary beads, and spoke with an acquired Queens, New York accent, peppered with her native Italian. Amidst the chatter of reporters, she hugged him. As mother and son embraced, tears streamed down their cheeks.

"I love you, baby. We're all so very proud. Your dad, God rest his soul, would have been so proud of his youngest." As she pondered what to say next, a smile crossed her face. "Your dad was constantly worried about a little boy who always wanted to cook. He thought it strange for a boy not to get out and fight a little," she said kissing him once again. "But when you wrote poetry for me, I knew there was more hope for you than that. I love you so much, my son," she said weeping openly. "You do what these people tell you, capish? They will make you well again. Everybody on our street is lighting candles for you in the church tonight," she continued, beginning to dry her eyes. "Father Lorenzo is saying a special Mass in your honor. I must go now. Be a good boy!" She kissed him one last time and said, "Good-bye, take care." The President took her by the arm and the entire entourage of reporters, generals, and Secret Service agents disappeared through the narrow hospital room door. The room again became quiet. He drifted off into a drug-induced sleep, lulled by the low-pitched whirring sound of the slowly rotating blades of an old wooden ceiling fan, endlessly turning above his bed.

He tossed and turned as if taunted by Satan himself. Sweat poured from his fevered brow. A secret locked deep inside his soul burned to get out. He was soon so overcome with his night-

A Star of Honor

mare, he cried out—tearing at his pillow as if it were alive and attacking him. Gentle hands shook him and he was abruptly snatched from his personal hell. "Come on now, wake up," said a soothing voice.

"Where am I?" She held him close and tried to console him. "I can't move my legs! Are they . . .?" She put her fingers lightly across his lips.

"No, they are there," she said in a soft, reassuring voice. "They are only sleeping, that's all. I'm a nurse, honey, and I should know. You want to talk about it?"

"No! There's nothing to talk about!"

"Please, Tony, talk to me. I want to help you," she said taking his hand and gently kissing it.

"How'd you know my name, anyway?"

"Look, Tony . . . here it is on your wristband. Why? Didn't you want me to know your name, handsome? Oh, I see! Italian, huh? Anthony Mag-na-ca-vello," she read cautiously. "Where 'ya from?"

"Queens, New York," he answered reluctantly.

"Tony, you must have done something really great!"

"Why do you say that?"

"Well, good-looking, it isn't everyday the President walks through that door to pin two medals on a patient. Well . . .? Aren't you going to tell me what you did?"

"No!," he answered sharply, abruptly jerking his arm from her grip. "I don't need these damn medals!" he yelled, almost screaming at her. "I ain't no damn hero! You understand?! Now leave me the hell alone. Just get the hell out of here and leave me alone!"

"All right!," she sobbed, visibly shaken, her eyes filling with tears. "I'll be here if you want to talk."

"I trust you," he replied, grabbing her hand before she left. "It's just very hard for me to talk about. I'm sorry for being such a jerk. Maybe later, okay?"

A Star of Honor

"All right," she answered, forcing a smile, "when you are ready." She covered him up again with a hospital blanket and softly said, "Sleep now, good-looking. Please try to get some rest."

After his heavy eyes followed her sleek, uniformed figure out the door, he dropped off to sleep.

Chapter 2

Once again, he tossed and turned in tortured agony, his blue hospital pajamas soaked with sweat. He lie there screaming obscenities at a now nonexistent Viet Cong enemy, still soundly asleep, but vividly replaying the drama over and over again.

"Tony!," screamed a frantic, female voice. "Wake up!" she persisted, shaking him, trying desperately to bring him back to reality. Finally, her efforts achieved a positive response. He quickly opened his eyes.

"What the hell is happening?"

"Tony, I heard you clear down the hall," she answered, now a bit calmer. "I really wasn't sure how to wake you, but I knew I had to." Taking his hand, she pressed it to her breasts.

"Thank you. I was back there again, in the land of gooks and rice," he said, trying to smile. "Oh . . . sorry!" he apologized, looking into her deep brown eyes. "I wasn't meaning anything towards you . . . understand?"

"Shush! I understand, good-looking, really I do. I lost a brother. He was killed in a Viet Cong ambush," she continued,

A Star of Honor

tears now visibly rolling down her cheeks. "I had to identify what was left of his body, so my family could bury him. I will never forget the horror in his eyes. . . ."

"What's your name?"

"Tia . . . Tia Gelita Ramos."

"I like you, Tia. You are good people."

"You want to talk now?"

"Maybe, Tia. Maybe I really have to talk this out . . ."

"But first, we put this I.V. tube back into your hand where it belongs!" She removed his hand from her breasts, and examined the small area of bright red ooze coming from the vein, with a deep concern. "You are going to be my problem patient, but I will still put up with you!" she said, producing a smile while gingerly applying alcohol and pushing the needle back into place. "There. This should hold it better," she said, applying an extra length of adhesive tape. "Now, you were saying?"

"Tell you the truth, I liked the nice warm place my hand was at a few minutes ago, much better than where it is now!"

"I really must talk to the doctor about those drugs. I think they have affected your brain!"

This room is too quiet, you know? Really sucks in here!"

"Well, good-looking, they only did it this way for the President's security. Also, your mama said she might be back to visit again, but she wasn't quite sure of the schedule. Are you feeling a little better now?"

"A little, Tia, but not a whole helluva lot. I kind of feel a bit like warmed over crapola. Would you come up here and sit next to me?"

"Airman! That is a no-no! Here, let me close this door. Don't tell anyone, okay?" she asked, while removing the doorstop and pushing the door closed.

"It will be our little secret. She then climbed up on the bed and sat down beside him. She readjusted the amounts of liquid slowly dripping down the long tube, protruding from his slightly

A Star of Honor

quivering hand. Tia placed another pillow behind him, and propped him up into a more comfortable position.

"Okay . . . now what?"

"Now . . . we talk."

She put her arms around him, being careful not to hurt him, and nestled his head against the softness of her breasts. She kicked off her white nurse's shoes, and let them drop to the floor, watching them land beneath the bed. She carefully readjusted her white dress, pulling the skirt down back over her almost exposed thigh. "There now, I'm a presentable captain again!" He didn't answer. She looked down, and felt a warm tear, which dropped from his eye onto her breast. She watched as he stared off into space. He seemed to be under a hypnotic spell, and began to sweat, starting to speak, as if he had no control. He clutched at her uniform and began to unravel. He started reliving his nightmare before her eyes. Now she started to understand better the plight of the troubled, battered, boy-turned-man she held in her arms.

"I was an airplane mechanic in Nam. I had been there for several months. I had managed to maintain a partial sanity up to that point, by drowning my sorrows with scotch and warm beer. Incoming rocket rounds were as inevitable as the sun coming up. Many times I had to dive for cover, as the Cong tried to hit our aircraft. Things got so bad, I carried a bottle of scotch around in my toolbox for emergencies," he continued, his mouth turning up at the corners in a slight smile. "At night, we took our pleasures when and where we could. You know what I mean . . . right?"

"I think so."

"What happened to me is a long and complicated story, but I will tell you what I remember. I was downtown at a bar, drinking my guts out . . . those pleasures, remember?"

"I remember, Tony. Go on," she coaxed.

"I sat in at a poker game. The smoke was so thick it burned the hell out of my eyes, and the music was so loud it numbed my ears. Above the smoke and confusion, I could see two half-naked Vietnamese women dancing in cages, suspended from the ceiling. I had won the last three hands," he recalled with a grin. "This Army grunt had lost it all to me. I said I needed an I.O.U., or something of value in the pot. He convinces me we need to go another hand, for all the marbles. So, he throws in this U.S. Government issued side arm. I looked it over . . . nice piece . . . Colt automatic. I let him throw it into the pot, with about four rounds. Up to then, all I ever carried was a good old New York switchblade. This pop-gun was really uptown! I took it from him as soon as I laid my cards down. He got so mad, he threw over the table. I broke a bottle over his cute, little grunt head. I took my winnings, and left. I dragged my tired, drunk bones back to the base. I went to the barracks, and dumped my ass in the bunk . . ."

"Sorry, Tony," Tia interrupted, "perhaps we can finish this later . . . I must make rounds now. But I promise, I will come back and we can continue, if you like."

"I really don't want you to go," he begged. She reluctantly climbed down from the bed and retrieved her shoes. She helped him lie back down and covered him again.

"I will be back around 2200, okay?"

"Okay, Tia . . . I won't sleep until you come back. I will wait."

"Okay," she reassured, kissing him on the forehead. "Save me a place on the bed, all right?"

"Sure will, ma'am."

Tia slipped her shoes back on and gathered her equipment. She readjusted her uniform, and started for the door. Tony was so deeply involved in thought, he did not see her leave. The room once again silent, but for the persistent whirring of the overhead fan. Then he realized she had gone. He lay in silence, with a war raging on in his brain, ever hopeful she would soon return.

Chapter 3

Tony waited as long as he could but his eyes grew heavy with fatigue, and he slowly drifted off into another world. The demons tormented him again. The lights flickered on and off in the hospital. He was startled by an enormous crash of thunder, which was soon followed by a flash of lightning, illuminating the night sky. He buried his head in his pillow and screamed, "Incoming! Incoming!," as torrents of rain poured down on the tin hospital roof, rekindling the fires of burning jungle memories. Friendly hands removed the pillow from his face, and he felt the soothing sensation of a cool, wet cloth, gently blotting up the sweat rolling down his cheeks and neck.

"Easy, good-looking. It was Tia, back from her rounds as promised. "Did you miss me, tough-guy?" she asked, as she adjusted the fluid's drip.

"Hell yes, mamma-san! How's about jumping back up here, and letting me finish?"

"Settle down now, Tony!" she said, kicking off her shoes, and climbing up next to him on the bed. "2200 is what I prom-

A Star of Honor

ised, and 2200 it is! Now, where were we? I believe you were dragging your tired, stinking, drunk bones back to the barracks."

"All right, smart-ass. If you aren't interested, I'll go back to sleep!"

"No, Tony. Please go on. I'm sorry." He stared out into space once more, and then continued to outpour the confines of his soul. She was the only woman, besides his mother, that to him was worthy of his trust.

"I was playing with my new toy while I was lying in bed. I kept pulling back the slide, then constantly clicking the hammer. I never owned a gun before, so it was fascinating for me. I was sipping a bit of Johnnie Walker Black, and listening to some tunes by Sonny and Cher. I was about to pass out, when I could hear off in the distance, what sounded like the flutter of birds. I heard those screams 'Incoming! Incoming!' We were all pretty well tuned into that sound. I rolled off the bed, just as the first rocket rounds hit the base. The Viet Cong always fired at night, hoping to hit the planes on the line, but the little fuckers never scored any hits on the aircraft, only the barracks area, and the rest of the compound. Keeping our minds numb with booze helped us deal with the fact that a stray round could flat-ass blow the shit out of us. Then, one of my worst fears happened. One of those gook bastards scored a big one on our barracks. I was flipped upside down, under my bunk . . ."

"Were you hurt?"

"There were casualties, but I was too fucking wasted to worry about it. The Security Police were firing back rounds, and tracers lit up the night like the Fourth of July. I watched from under my mattress. I tried to block out the sounds of the wounded, and their painful screaming with my pillow . . ." Tony clutched the sheets tightly in both hands, his body quivered with fear. His pajamas were drenched as he tried to continue describing the aftermath. "I suppose, I was the lucky one . . . but I ain't sure yet about that," he said, somewhat regaining his compo-

A Star of Honor

sure. "All I could see around me were airmen with their bodies ripped to hell. I was in shock and couldn't move to help anyone. I probably wouldn't have anyway. 'Long as it wasn't me that got hit, I really didn't give a shit. Honest, tia, I really didn't." She placed two fingers over his lips, and tried to calm him.

"Tony, slow down a bit, tiger. I will be getting off shift soon, and I've got to get the ward ready for the change." She gave him a shot of morphine, and softly kissed his forehead. "Rest now, good-looking. Tomorrow's another day. Do you still want to talk about it?"

"Well, I got nothing but time."

"Me too, baby. Me too," she said, climbing down off the bed once again. "Good-night, good-looking."

"Good-night, Tia. Thanks for listening."

"I'll be back tomorrow, Tony. Take care." She picked up her shoes, and walked in stocking-feet towards the door. As lightning cast long, eerie shadows on the hospital room wall, Tony watched Tia's silhouette disappear into the darkness, and allowed himself to be lulled to sleep by the sweet music of the rain, and the contentment of morphine.

Chapter 4

After a long, hot and humid Philippine night, and following the onslaught of a monsoon storm, an exhausted Tony lie in bed. He gladly welcomed the ray of sunlight, peeking through a slight space in the bamboo shade covering his window.

An orderly brought in a tray of breakfast, and set it on a stand in front of him. He stared at it, sitting just above the legs he could not feel. The bed was cranked up, putting him into a sitting position. The orderly wheeled his cart, heaped with other breakfast trays, through the narrow doorway and out into the hall. He turned to Tony on his way out and mumbled, "Have a nice day."

An American Air Force doctor entered, followed by a group of new orderlies. They were learning the rounds of the ward, and were getting familiar with the patients. The doctor was a major, his gold leaves visible on the collar protruding from his long, white hospital coat. A stethoscope hung from around his neck, precariously dangling from side to side, like a silver Christmas tree ornament. His blond hair was cut short, into a flat-top, and he wore Air Force issued, black-framed glasses. His name tag

A Star of Honor

read: JACOBSON. Tony wondered where he had seen that name before. Major Jacobson removed Tony's chart from the bed and pondered it thoughtfully before speaking. Tony was now struggling to lift a fork-full of scrambled, powdered eggs and a piece of meat resembling sausage, to his lips. He dropped bits of it onto the clean white sheet below.

"You were the guy they brought in a few days ago, right? Frankly, pal, I didn't think you would last through the night, let alone this long. I got some bad news for you, hero. Looks like you won't be walking again . . . ever. Sorry about that." He looked up from the chart as though he didn't have a care in the world and continued with his callous speech. "A bullet shattered against your spine, and that is why you're paralyzed from below the waist. Tough luck, pal." Tony's face grew red with anger. He took his food tray and threw it against the wall, narrowly missing the frantically ducking orderlies.

"So, you're the asshole who wrote me off!" "You call yourself a doctor? You're a fucking fool!" He yanked out the long tube attached to the top of his hand and grabbed the doctor around the neck, as he leaned over him. Tony squeezed with every ounce of strength he had. The orderlies, all at once, tried to separate his grip from Jacobson's neck. The doctor's face turned a purple hue from a lack of oxygen as Tony tried his best to strangle him.

"Stop, Tony! Stop!" came a concerned, familiar voice. "Tony, let him go!" It was Tia. She was wearing a long, flowered, and brightly colored cotton Philippine dress with white sandals. Her long shiny black hair was flowing freely and hanging down over her shoulders. She was off duty but had decided to spend her free time with Tony, a man who provoked her curiosity and had accepted her friendship. She looked on in utter disbelief at what was happening.

"Tony, turn him loose right now! That's an order, airman!" Tony reluctantly let go, still in a fit of anger. "Dr. Jacobson, what the hell is happening? What are you doing to this patient?" Jacob-

A Star of Honor

son, now gasping to regain his breath, said, "This nut tried to kill me!"

"Nut indeed, doctor! Get the hell away from him or I will take great pleasure in putting my dainty Filipino foot straight up your ass! Orderly . . . call the Security Police!"

"Yes, ma'am!" snapped one of the airmen, dressed in a neatly pressed, starched-white uniform.

"But he tried to kill me! He called me an asshole! I'll have him brought up on charges . . ."

"Like hell, you will! I was there when you declared him dead! We should have *you* up on charges! Now get out of here! While you're at it, major, you might as well file charges on me too. But right now, you had better leave before I really lose my temper!" The doctor staggered to the door, with one hand on the orderly, and the other stroking his throat, which was now rubbed raw.

"This is not finished yet, captain!" he shouted at Tia.

"Go on, get out of here! And oh yes, major . . . you *are* an asshole!" Then looking at Tony, "I knew you would be my problem child, but this is ridiculous!" She smiled as she carefully replaced the tube back into his hand and fluffed up his pillow. "I see you redecorated our walls with your scrambled eggs too. I don't call this taking in nourishment! My god, Tony. What am I going to do with you?"

"Guess you are stuck with me, nurse," he said. "And by the way, lady . . . you ain't half bad for a fucking officer!"

"You ain't half bad yourself, good-looking . . . for an enlisted puke! Now try and get some rest, okay?"

"Okay. But only for you."

"I'll see you later, Tony."

"Okay, mamma-san . . . later!" Tia left and Tony reflected on what he had done. He stared out the window through the

A Star of Honor

small space in the bamboo shade. He did what Tia ordered, and tried to get some sleep.

Chapter 5

Tony slept most of the day, with the exception of an occasional interruption by busy orderlies. He watched amused, as they scurried, reminding him of busy little wind-up dolls in white suits. One orderly, barely old enough to shave, stared at him. He wore only one stripe on his neatly pressed whites. He had blue eyes and short-cropped red hair; his face was covered with freckles.

"Are you the hero?"

"What the hell do you want, kid?"

"I just wanted to see you, that's all. The whole place is buzzing about you! Did you kill a lot of gooks?"

"Kid, I ain't done shit! Now get the hell out of here!"

"But . . ."

"Just do your job, and get the hell out of here, you little asshole!"

"The young airman started for the door. He turned towards Tony's bed and said, "God forgives you for being nasty, and so do I. Take care, hero. Jesus loves you." Then he quickly left.

A Star of Honor

Tony thought, 'Just what I need, a hippie Jesus-freak in a white suit! This has got to be my lucky day!'

The day nurse, a young lieutenant with pinned up blond hair, strolled in. "Well, good-afternoon, airman," she said, trying to be cheerful. Due to lack of experience, she nervously fumbled with his chart and attempted to take his pulse and temperature. She then administered the exact dosage of medication the chart called for. Her blue eyes peered over her wire-framed glasses which slipped down over her nose. "My name is Sam . . . short for Samantha, that is. I have strict orders from Captain Ramos to take good care of you!"

"Where is she?"

"Don't worry, baby, she'll be here soon."

"Look, lieutenant!" he snapped. "If you want to get along with me, remember two things: I ain't worried about nothing, and I ain't your baby! So don't let the door hit you in the ass on the way out!"

Unaffected, she casually strolled back out the door. Tony wondered how long he could endure the solitude of being alone in his misery.

Soon the sun, like a bright red fireball, began setting across the passionate Philippine sky. He listened to the sounds of the streets off in the distance, and could faintly distinguish the cries of street vendors hawking their wares to the unsuspecting, slightly inebriated G.I.s on leave. He could barely see from his window, the outlines of palm trees swaying to the gentle humid breezes, which would soon usher in the fall of darkness once again.

He wished he could be a part of it all as he had been, in the not too distant past. His tenacity and raw courage learned in the streets of New York, would not let him succumb to the doctor's diagnosis of never walking again. In all of his eighteen years, he would always fight for what he believed in and would never give up on any endeavor he pursued. He had come too far, and had

A Star of Honor

been through too much, to give up on it now.

Tony yearned for Tia's company. He counted the hours that would return her to his bedside. He hoped he would be able to stay awake until she came back on shift. The gentle softness of her touch remained constant in his thoughts. Most of all, he wanted to swallow his Italian pride and thank her with a simple kiss for coming to his defense earlier. He wanted to continue to share with her the many suppressed secrets hidden deep in the labyrinth of his anguished mind.

Chapter 6

Hours passed slowly. Work shifts finally changed again. The roar of jets could be heard across the base coming from the flightline. The mighty Air Force F-4 fighter planes were being readied; their freshly armed payloads of destruction destined for the communist occupants of North Vietnam.

Mechanics and munitions maintenance personnel worked around the clock. They kept the aircraft in a constant state of readiness. The U.S. aircrews in their camouflaged chariots, constantly shattered the serenity of the peaceful Philippine countryside. Each night, scores of missions to "The Nam" blasted off into the moonlit skies; with courses charted towards uncertainty, many would never return.

"What's up, good-looking?" sounded the voice Tony longed for. "Have no fear, your favorite nurse is here! Did you miss me? You really don't have to answer that 'ya know!"

"I did miss you, Tia! Nobody fusses over me like you do!"

"Oh stop it! Just doing my job," she said checking his chart and straightening his covers. "Have you been behaving yourself

A Star of Honor

in my absence, or have you strangled any more doctors lately?"

"Shit, Tia! That's so funny, I forgot to laugh!"

"Aw, come on, Tony. Where's your sense of humor tonight? Besides, I brought you something, if you feel up to it."

"Shit, lady! I hope it's something to eat! I don't think I can handle any more pussy today!"

"Now who's being funny?" she scolded playfully. "I brought you some Filipino barbecued chicken. If you would like to have some, I will help you . . . would you?"

"Sure, mama-san, anything is better than the slop they serve in this joint . . . Jesus Christ! You call that chicken? Looks like it got run over by a bus or something!"

"Tony, just shut up and eat, or I swear, I will never bring another thing for you . . . ever!"

"Sorry, Tia. Guess my day has been shitty all around."

"Well, join the party! Say, are you going to hog all that run-over chicken?"

Tony munched away and wished he could wash it down with the warm beer he had grown accustomed to back at the air base in Vietnam. Tia jumped up on the bed as though it were her rightful place to be. "Move it or lose it, airman!" she said as she giggled. Her shoes flew in opposite directions as she snuggled in close to Tony. "You like my cooking?"

"It's very good!" said Tony, licking the barbecue sauce from his fingers. "Sure could use a San Miguel right now!"

"I didn't realize you liked Philippine beer! But . . . since I already broke the rules with the chicken . . ." Tia then reached down into a woven straw bag she carried the chicken in, and produced a small brown glass bottle of San Miguel. She removed the bottle cap and handed it to Tony. "Just a few sips, good-looking, and keep your big mouth shut about it!" Tony took a few sips and slowly savored each mouthful. He let it glide down his throat and just grinned with contentment.

"Hell, mamma-san, I'll marry you for a bottle of Johnnie

A Star of Honor

Walker Black!"

"Nice try, Mr. Shithead!" The smile then left her face and she asked Tony if he wanted to talk about what was troubling him. He nodded, as she dabbed at the barbecue sauce on his face with a napkin. Tony lay back and looked into Tia's big brown eyes. He beckoned her to come closer. When she was close enough, he kissed her lightly on the cheek.

"What was that all about?"

"Just my way of saying thanks for defending my honor today," he said with a red face.

"Oh, Tony! You are very sweet . . . for a pain in the ass!" She kissed his forehead and said, "I know you would do the same for me. So, where were we with our conversation?" Tony's face turned to a serious frown, as he began to recall the intense happenings of Vietnam.

Chapter 7

"Long after the attack on the base, I was still shaking all over. The medics and the search teams were digging through the rubble of what used to be my home away from home. Fifteen people got blown away that night! Eight others wound up gimps like me. But . . . however . . . I made it through that one without a scratch!"

"You were lucky!"

"Hell, lucky? Baby, I led a charmed life over there! I always came out of scrapes smelling like a rose!"

"Kind of like a cat."

"Yeah . . . nine lives, that's it exactly" said the New York Italian, with a grin. "But I guess I'd have trouble landing on my feet now, huh?"

"Oh, Tony, hush! I pray for you every night. I just know things will go your way. Mark my words!"

"Why doesn't that make me feel any better, Tia?"

"What happened after that?"

"Well . . . I needed to get out of there real bad, so I hitched a

A Star of Honor

ride downtown with some grunts passing by in a jeep. I went back to my favorite night spot . . . The Jade Dragon. The music invited me in from the hot, filth-ridden street. I entered the smoke-filled den and strolled up to the bar. I sat down on a round vinyl stool, and resumed the drowning of my sorrows. A Vietnamese bar girl, named Shin Lee, asked me to buy her a drink. After three drinks she wanted to take me home, so I left the bar with her. I was really fucked up . . . but you have to understand . . . I really had no place to sleep that night . . ."

"No need to justify things Tony. I understand . . . really I do."

"This chick was really dressed to kill! She had on a low-cut green mini-dress with thin shoulder straps. Her hair was long and black like yours. She wore a pearl necklace and green shoes. She grabbed onto my arm, and we strolled out into the blackness of the misty night." Tia remained silent as Tony went on with his awkward, but detailed story. "We went walking through the many winding back alleys of the city, clotheslines and laundry hung everywhere. People were cooking in the streets, and the stink of fish and stuff burning was blowing up my nose!"

"Okay! I get the picture!" Tia snapped, wondering just how much Tony would tell her about this experience.

"Soon we came to the street she was looking for. I followed the chick up a flight of stairs in a run-down, flophouse hotel. I could hear people chattering . . . like so many slant-eyed chipmunks! Babies were crying and crawling around the halls unattended. This joint really stunk! We came to a room at the end of the hallway. She pulled out a small room key that was safely tucked between her tits, cautiously stuck it in the keyhole and turned it until the door opened. I followed her in as she turned on some black lights, and lit a stick of incense in a small brass ashtray, with a long wooden stick match she retrieved from among many others standing in an old mayonnaise jar. The sweet smell of jasmine and cheap perfume captivated my senses.

A Star of Honor

She wanted five bucks. I felt it was too much . . . but I gave it up anyway. I fell back on the bed and watched as she unzipped the dress and let it slowly drop. Then, I just couldn't believe what I saw next!" Tia nodded and motioned with her eyes for Tony to go on. "I pulled back the torn, smelly spread on the bed and found two Vietnamese children . . . little girls. They were scared; I could see them shaking with fear. They were crying and called out to their mother. She told them to shut up! As she spoke to them in Vietnamese, I just couldn't believe this was happening."

"Then what?"

"I couldn't hold back my tears as I looked into their frightened little faces. I just knew they were starving," he said, as tears rolled down his cheeks. "I saw a part of Nam that night that I guess . . . I just overlooked until then. The mother stood there naked in front of me and her kids. I jumped up and covered her with that dress. I pulled a hundred dollars from my wallet and made her take it. I hugged the two little girls and begged the mother to use the money for them. I told her to stay home with her kids that night. She cried and tried to kiss me, but I gently pushed her away and stumbled out the door and down the stairs. I drag-bagged back to the base, just in time to grab a cold shower and go to work . . ."

Tia saw something in Tony that night she hadn't seen before. She wasn't quite sure what it was, but she was sure she liked it. She poured some of the warm San Miguel left into a glass. Tia first allowed Tony to sip the beer slowly, before taking a sip herself. As they shared what was left, they became lost together, deep in silent thought.

Chapter 8

Tony and Tia drifted off into a peaceful sleep; they lie side by side on the narrow hospital bed. Tony felt a sense of security snuggled in the softness of Tia's arms. Suddenly, his body began to quiver as he shouted obscenities. Tia was awakened by the noise and knew immediately what was happening. She tried to shake him without hurting the many wounds he sustained. Finally, with no response, she threw a glass of water on him and he was snatched quickly from his terror.

"What?"

"Easy, good-looking, calm down. Please, Tony, let it go!" she reassured, as she hugged him close to her body. "Talk to me. Talk to me! Please wake up!"

"Okay, I'm awake!"

"Tony, my god, tell me what it was. It seemed so terrible. You poor baby. Get it out. Please, talk to me." Tony stared off into space as he tried to recall his dream. "It happened when I was on temporary duty to the base at Nha Trang. Mechanics were moved up and down the country, when and wherever needed due to mission requirements. I used to make my gambling money by selling a few things downtown. 'Ya know what I mean?"

"We call that the Black Market, in the Philippines."

"Exactly! Same-same in 'The Nam.' Seems like the Vietnamese people had this strange fascination with American supplies. They especially liked American jungle boots. Why? I ain't got a clue. But it was big bucks in the wallet for whoever had them to sell. I crew-chiefed all the transient aircraft that flew in so I had a first-hand look at all the potential merchandise."

"Go on . . ."

"Well . . . I found out through the grapevine, we called it the "rice-line," that a shipment was coming on the next C-130 cargo plane inbound for servicing. I was already counting the money as the tower cleared it to land."

"You were not a very nice guy, huh, Tony? But they do it here in my country too, so it's no problem!"

"Right! You want to hear this or not?"

"Please, go on."

"Well, the airplane taxied in and I martialed it to its parking area. It was only here for the servicing, so I figured I'd better work fast. I thought it was funny for a C-130 not to open its back cargo door. This one didn't . . . and I wondered why."

"Was that unusual?"

"Very unusual, baby! I stuck the big wooden chocks under the wheels so she wouldn't roll, and watched as the crew departed. I pulled the forms from the maintenance folder, and began reading the check list. I just couldn't get my mind off that cargo I was about to get my hands on! I climbed up the small ladder on the left side of the aircraft, and entered through the doorway. It was hotter than hell in there! Without the cargo door open, it was kind of dark. Something nasty, combined with the intense heat, created a really bad smell that just about knocked me out. Something was very strange about this cargo. I pulled a

27

flashlight from my tool bag, and began my search of the contents. I first climbed the ladder up to the flight deck. I wanted to see if the crew had left behind any good paperbacks or *Playboy* books," he grinned slyly. "Just wasn't having much luck in that respect though. The stink in that airplane about made me gag. I jumped in the pilot-seat, and played pilot for a while . . . like I used to do when I was a kid. After I was through amusing myself, I climbed down and made my way past the radio operator's compartment. Then . . . what I saw, will I'm sure, haunt me for the rest of my life." Tia stared wide-eyed at Tony, and wondered what was coming next. "Brown zipper-bags were hanging on hooks all around the walls of the cargo compartment. The bags had loops for handles on them and reminded me of clothing bags. They covered the round portholes of the aircraft. I guess that's why it was so dark. I still wasn't really sure what I had there, so I shined my light on the cargo stacked up in the back. I saw metal crates with handles on the sides, stacked on top of one another. Each was draped with an American flag, and each stack was tied down like the cargo next to it. I knew this was the first stop for those about to take their last journey home."

"Tony, I know the feeling," said Tia, her eyes filling with tears. "My brother was returned the same way when he was killed at Pleiku. Please go on."

"I examined the bags hanging on the side walls a bit closer and saw the label: BODY PARTS. I counted twenty bags . . . ten on each wall. I turned and wanted to get out of there! I tripped over a tie-down strap and fell on the deck of the aircraft. I landed close to a hammock in the down-position. The shock of reality hit me like a round-house punch! There were bodies lying on all the hammocks, covered with bloody sheets . . ." he sighed and continued on. "I felt as though they might have been bodies fresh from a battle or something. Perhaps even some were from my own barracks. I just wasn't sure. I picked up one of the sheets so that I would know I wasn't dreaming. Then it happened! One of

A Star of Honor

the bodies sat up! His face was half blown-off and he had no arms! His eyes seemed to look straight into mine! His mouth opened and he let out a belch. I was terrified! The body fell back onto the hammock, and I bolted for the door as fast as my legs would carry me. I fell down twice more trying to get outside. I dove through the hatchway and down onto the ground with a very hard landing on my ass. I sat there just looking at the brown and green camouflaged *carrier of death.*"

"Tony, you do understand there was nothing supernatural about the body rising?" asked Tia, trying to share her medical expertise with the obviously shaken, young airman. "The body was getting rid of excess gas. They sometimes do that . . . rise and belch, I mean."

"Tia! That is not the point! When I saw all those bodies all at once, I actually started to realize how this good-for-nothing war was butchering our people! In fact, I could have been a sack of meat when they hit the barracks!"

"Stop it, Tony! Just stop it!" she said, practically screaming at him. "What did you do after that?"

"I just picked myself up and ran and ran, until I couldn't run any more. I thought about what I had witnessed, and puked my guts out. I went to the airman's club and drank 'till I couldn't stand up."

"Rest now, good-looking, please rest . . . okay?"

"It hurts, Tia!" he yelled. "Shoot me up, Tia! Please . . . I need a shot . . . it hurts so bad!" Tia jumped off the bed and ran out of the room. She quickly came back with morphine to calm him. She injected it into his arm and peace quickly came over him. Tony fell off into the realm of sleep once again. Tia covered him and kissed his forehead. "Sleep, good-looking. I'm here for you, when you need to talk again." She adjusted his I.V. bottle and picked up her shoes. She quietly slipped out of the room and returned to her busy hospital duties.

Chapter 9

Tony lie in a deep state of tranquility. The cool, gentle breezes of night, drifted off into obscurity. The stars and moon were soon overpowered by the many brilliant multi-colored rays of sunlight. The light seemed to peek into every corner of the room. It created a rustic beauty over the land as well. Streaks of color were painted in illusion over the horizon; a scene of serenity was reflected upon the busy city and rice paddies below.

Tia was totally exhausted. She spent most of the night running from room to room, applying her full attentions specifically to the needs of others. The caring she administered to her patients, grew out of unselfish love and her strict devotion to duty. The young Filipino nurse of twenty-three, sat in a chair close by Tony's bed. She gazed silently at his majestic profile. Tia watched, as his aura seemed to settle into a dreamless, peaceful state of well-being. She wondered about the tragedies and horrors he witnessed. How long would the truth about Tony Magnacavello stay locked up deep inside his tortured soul? What could he possibly have done, to have everyone refer to him as a

A Star of Honor

hero? She thought to herself, 'My god! The President of the United States of America was here, and on my ward too! He came all the way from Washington, D.C., just to pin a medal on this broken, battered boy, from Queens, New York!

As the first light of day seemed to dance upon his eyes, Tony was awakened to the sweet smell of perfume. It tantalized his senses. He looked to see if the scent belonged to Tia, and much to his delight, it did. "Well, good-morning, you sweet, little brown Filipino baby!" he grinned, acting quite proud of his remark.

"Oh, that was cute! So, you wouldn't let me sneak out of here without saying good-bye, huh?"

"Why, hell no, mamma-san! Nobody sneaks out on me . . . especially not beautiful women!"

"Oh? And just what exactly does a little boy know of beautiful women?" she replied, now taking her turn to smile, catching his Italian pride completely off guard.

"Okay, you win!" In a noble manner, he bestowed a good-morning kiss on top of her hand. "Hmmm . . . soft," he said, his deep brown eyes now focusing on hers. "What the hell are you still doing here anyway?" he inquired, squeezing her hand playfully.

"They are bringing you a roommate today, good-looking. I am here to make sure you are a good little boy when he arrives. I really want you to behave too! Do you hear me, airman?"

"Well, *fuck*, Tia. What the hell makes him so special?"

"Tony, now stop it! Do you hear me? All of you are special to me. *You*, of all people, should know that. When he gets here, you will be nice to him or else!"

"Or else what, tough-lady?"

"Or else I will cut off your ration of San Miguel!"

"Aw, shit. You got me with that one all right. Okay! I'll be good . . . I promise."

"Tony, I wonder why, in the back of my sweet, little Filipino

31

A Star of Honor

mind, I just don't believe you! Quit acting so jealous, good-looking."

"Jealous?!" he screamed, Italian pride now surfacing again. "And just what is it that you think would make me jealous?"

"Oh, Tony, hush now, okay? The important thing is the two of you get along. You might as well make room in your heart for at least one more friend in your life, besides me. One just never knows about these things. Please try to keep an open mind!"

"I never was very big on friends, Tia, and I really don't care to have that many now. I really do promise to be good . . . but only out of respect for you," he answered, with a great degree of belligerence.

"Okay, any way you want to do it. And oh yes . . . thanks, good-looking!" she winked, then gently kissed his forehead and turned to leave. "See 'ya later."

"Okay, baby . . . later," he answered.

Tia quickly slipped away so she could supervise the arrival of his soon-to-be roommate. Tony wondered what this new roommate would be like. He pretended to be sleeping, as an orderly brought in a breakfast tray. Another boring, ritualistic day in the life of a so-called hero.

Chapter 10

Soon the monotony of hospital life changed. The door pushed open; Tia and Samantha wheeled in a sleeping patient. This was his new roommate. "Hi, ladies!" said Tony, pretending to be sweet. "What the hell you got there?"

"Now, Tony, remember what you promised!"

"Okay, okay, no biggie. I'll be good! What's *his* problem anyway?"

"Well, he is sedated now, but will be coming out of it in a few hours," disclosed Tia. "He's a double-amputee, and that adjustment will not be an easy one." Tia and Samantha carefully moved the big, muscle-bound man into his bed.

"Put him by the door!" demanded Tony. "I get the window! That's all I look forward to in this shithole, so I get the window!"

"Relax, good-looking, you can keep the window . . . for now."

"What the hell do you mean . . . for now?"

Samantha took over the lecture. "Look here, hot-shot. This man is a Marine, flown in late last night. They weren't able to

A Star of Honor

take him at the Army hospital on Okinawa. He may only be with us for a short while before they move him. He just lost both his legs, damnit! You will be as nice to him as possible! Besides, he's a sergeant, and outranks you, airman! You got all that?"

"Tia! Tell that blonde person I got all that . . . if she got all *this*!" he screamed, as he pointed his middle finger at her in an obscene gesture.

"Both of you, stop this. What do I have to do? Stay here twenty-four hours a day just to referee all of your exhibition fights, Tony? She was very obviously annoyed with what was going on. "As for you, lieutenant, I will see you in my office as soon as we secure this patient."

"Yes, ma'am." She knew at that moment, getting Tia angry was a bad idea.

"Tia, get that stinking jarhead out of my room!"

"Tony! You shut up right now! I don't want any more crap out of you, or I will tape up your mouth . . . I swear I will!"

"Oh swell, pick on a defenseless cripple, right? That's just great, Tia."

"Tony, that wasn't fair, and it hurt."

"Well, you started it, mamma-san!"

"Tony, I have nothing more to say to you right now. Don't say anything, okay?" Her eyes began to tear. She finished her work and started for the door, motioning for Samantha to follow.

"Sorry I pissed you off, Tia."

"Just be quiet," she pleaded. "I am getting out of here before I say something we both will be sorry for later. I'll be back tonight. I'm sorry for getting angry with you. I was very unprofessional, and a friend shouldn't react that way."

"But, Tia . . ."

"No, Tony, don't talk to me . . . not now. I must go and cool down. I really like you, Tony . . . but sometimes your words cut my heart like a knife." She turned and quickly went to the door, almost running. She tried to contain her tears, but couldn't. She

A Star of Honor

never turned back to say good-bye. Tia left, followed out the door by a very worried Samantha.

Tony knew he had made a mess of things. He knew he had hurt his only friend. "There goes my Johnnie Walker Black!" he remarked. "Magnacavello, you really fucked up this time!" He lay back and just looked at the big Marine next to him. "Well big guy, I guess it's just you and me . . . whoever the fuck you are." He was totally sure at that point, it wasn't going to be a very nice day. "If that carrot-topped hippie comes back and says that to me . . . I'll strangle the sonuvabitch!" He regained his composure, and again reflected on what he had done.

Chapter 11

Tony stared at the sleeping Marine for hours. The man groaned as he awoke from his sedated condition. He was calling out to his imaginary comrades. It sounded like he might have been repeating map grid coordinates for an air strike. "We need some hits here! On my mark! Charlie's taking over this position! Can not hold! REPEAT! CAN NOT HOLD this position! We're getting out of Dodge! Time to di-di-mow!" Tony frantically kept pushing the emergency call-button, attached to the rail on his bed. Samantha ran into the room, with two orderlies in hot pursuit.

"What's going on in here?"

"Give this guy a shot or something, Sam! He's really freaking out! He must have dropped some bad acid!"

"Can you hear me? MARINE! WAKE UP!"

"Fuck, Sam, what are you practicing to be? A drill sergeant?"

"Shut up, Tony! Have you got any better ideas? Besides, you got me in enough trouble as it is. Because of you, Captain Ramos took a big piece of my ass!"

A Star of Honor

"Hell, Sam, with the ass you got . . . you could afford to lose some of it!"

"Not now, hot-shot!" she snapped. "This is serious!" She shook the hysterical Marine until he seemed to regain consciousness. She jabbed him quickly with the needle one of the orderlies handed her. It brought him into a relaxed state. It was only then, she and the orderlies were able to return to their other duties. The Marine stared out into space, clearly lost in his own world. His brown hair was cut so short, only a tuft of it could be seen on top of his head. The hair just above his ears was shaved clean. He was weary, as was evident by the dark circles under his brown eyes. A heavy beard stubble was beginning to appear on his deeply suntanned face. "What is this place?"

"This is a hospital, buddy! Do you remember your name?"

"I . . . I think so . . . yes, it's Mike. Mike Matheson, U.S.M.C.! My rank is sergeant, and I'm the meanest motherfucker in the corps! I killed so many of them little yellow termites, that Hanoi put a ten-thousand dollar bounty on my head . . . dead or alive! By the way . . . you can call me Spike!"

"Okay, Spike. You can call me Tony, and I'm the meanest motherfucker in Queens! I got to admit though, those are some beautiful tattoos you got there." Tony was eyeing the many colorful markings etched on both of the big Marine's arms.

"You like 'em? I got most of 'em on R and R (rest and relaxation) back on Okinawa. I was drunker than shit, or else I wouldn't have gotten them. I like my bulldog the best!" he boasted, pointing out the tattoo on his left tricep muscle. It was a picture of a bulldog's head wearing a Marine fatigue cap. Just below it were scrawled the initials: USMC. Its mouth moved everytime he flexed his bulging muscles. "So, how long you in for, Tony?"

"Well, Spike . . . I guess for the duration. I can't use my legs anymore."

"That's a bummer, Tony! Say, where'd you get that *fruit salad*, anyway? What'd you do, knock over the PX?" he smiled,

A Star of Honor

eluding to the two military medals hanging from the pocket of Tony's hospital pajamas.

"Nothing to it! I don't know why I got them. I ain't done shit!"

"Bullshit, man!" interrupted the arrogant Marine. "That little hummer is a Silver Star! I would have killed my own grandmother for one of those! Why, shit! One day back in gook-land, I had to hold off a Viet Cong human-wave attack that tried to overrun our position. I hammered away with an M-60 machine gun and grenades for damn near three hours. I directed friendly fire on my position to get Charlie off my men. My guys scattered in all directions! I ran for it when I saw everyone was out of there and in the clear. Army choppers strafed my position on the coordinates I radioed in. The VC tried to take me out with mortar rounds. I must have stepped on a live mine in the rice paddy I was running through . . . or hit a trip-wire to a grenade booby trap. The explosion is all I can remember. Hell, I ain't even got a Silver Star!"

"Maybe it got held up in paperwork. I don't deserve mine. You could probably use it better than I could."

"Hell no, flyboy! They don't just hand those out! I'm truly impressed! This is my ticket home across the pond, buddy!" quipped the Marine, referring to his wounds. "When I get back to the world, I'll try out for the Olympics once again. I was a long distance runner . . . before I joined the corps, that is!"

Tony knew at that moment Spike hadn't been told about his legs being amputated below the knees. He wasn't sure if he should be the one to break the news. 'This jarhead could trip out and try to kill me or something,' he thought. 'Legs or not . . . he's built like a goddamn monster! I think I better take it easy on this dude!'

"Yeah, Spike, that's cool all right. The Olympics is what you need to do . . . if you're that good at it!" Tony suggested, trying to humor him.

At that moment, Major Jacobson entered the room, check-

A Star of Honor

ing patients as he made his rounds. 'Oh fuck!' thought Tony. 'There goes the neighborhood, and here goes my happy fucking home!'

Chapter 12

"Well, now I got two of you to put up with," remarked Jacobson. "First, an airman street-punk with a bad attitude, and now . . . a jarhead with an even worse attitude!"

"Don't listen to this guy, Spike. Whatever he says to you . . . well . . . I'd damn sure get a second opinion!" Jacobson began examining the Marine, hastily jotting down his findings.

"Well, doc? Am I gonna live?" joked Spike. Jacobson peered over his glasses, ignoring what was being said. He put the ends of his stethoscope into his ears and listened to Spike's heartbeat. "Well, doc . . . you can send me back to duty any time now! What do you think?"

"Back to duty! Ha! Doing what?" came the major's cruel response. "Jarhead, you'll be lucky to get a ticket back to the world to sell pencils on a street corner and carry a tin cup!"

"Don't listen to him, Spike! This guy is a fucking lunatic! Major . . . I used to have a pet cockroach that you remind me a lot of. You want to know what happened to it?"

"All right, Magnacavello, what happened to it?"

A Star of Honor

"Well, I used to watch it do tricks every day in the jar it lived in . . ."

"And I suppose there's some sort of moral to all this, you little scumbag?"

"Right! When I quit being amused by it . . . I simply stomped the living dogshit out of it, or should I say roachshit?" Both patients laughed out loud at Jacobson's expense. Tony hoped the sadistic doctor would go away and let things calm down. Jacobson became infuriated at the two new roommates' laughter.

"Very funny! Such witty words . . . coming from a couple of legless wonders!"

"What the fuck's he mean, legless wonders?" asked Spike, concern in his voice. "I'll get up and pound him to a pulp!"

"Right, jarhead. You need to catch me first . . . but you've got to have something to stand on before you can do that!" snarled Jacobson, in a content tone of voice.

"Sheesh," Tony thought aloud. "The shit dun-hit-da-fan now!" Spike looked at Jacobson.

"You mean . . . I ain't got no legs, major?"

"Now you get it, sucker! They were amputated when we had you on the table . . . early this morning."

"You son-of-a-bitch! I should have fucking killed you when I had the chance!" Tony grabbed a lamp from the small green nightstand standing by his bed. He began swinging it around wildly, trying desperately to hit Jacobson with it.

"I hope you two tough assholes will be very happy together," he smirked. He began moving towards the door at a rapid pace just as the lamp Tony was swinging crashed into a million glass and metal pieces. It hit the wall just above the fleeing doctor's head, as he narrowly escaped.

"Next time, I'll kill you! You come back here . . . and I'll kill you! I swear on my mother!" Tony looked over at Spike. "You all right, man?" Spike didn't answer. The impact of Jacobson's words kept re-sounding over and over in the Marine's mind. All

A Star of Honor

the fighting spirit had drained from his now seemingly lifeless body.

"I guess I bought the big one, 'eh?"

"Hey, man, what the fuck? Be glad you ain't dead!" Spike considered Tony's evaluation.

"Maybe getting killed . . . wasn't such a bad idea after all," he mumbled in a depressed tone of voice.

Tony shook his head and wondered about what kind of future would be in store for both he and Spike, and how to cope with his problems, now complicated more than ever, by a crazy doctor who could care less if they lived or died.

Chapter 13

After the passing of several long humid weeks, Tony and Spike became the best of friends. Tia kept a constant vigil over both, as though pretending to be their mother. During that time, Tony was wheeled to the operating room once again. Doctors tried in vain, to remove some of the remaining bullet fragments still lodged in his back. In the days to follow, Tony would be forced to start over, on a long agonizing journey down the increasingly rough road to recovery. Spike plunged into the deepest depths of depression. He was never able to fully accept the reality of the untimely loss of his legs.

The two patients lie in their beds, with nothing to do but read and listen to the radio. The newspaper they read, *The Pacific Stars and Stripes*, was the only officially sanctioned source of news available to the U.S. Forces in Southeast Asia. That, and the *Life* magazines Tia brought them, offered nothing more than grim reminders of the blazing war they left behind.

An Armed Forces radio station was playing all the current rock 'n roll hits popular in the states. They listened to the scratchy

A Star of Honor

voice of a well-known disk jockey, whose radio shows were taped and sent to the Pacific Theatre of Operations. The music filled their heads with thoughts and dreams of home . . . which now seemed to be a million miles away. An older release by Elvis, calmed the men and soothed their restless souls, but did nothing to ease the constant pain they suffered. Tony became more and more dependent on daily drug injections, and Spike just didn't care anymore.

"Yo, Spike! How the hell are you?"

"Who's there?" answered Spike, still groggy.

"Shit, sarge! You forgot about us already?"

"Well, hell's bells! Who let you wimps in here?"

"What's going on?" asked Tony, now wide awake.

"Look at this, Tony. It's my goddamned buddies from Danang!" Excitement appeared on the face of the big Marine.

"Damn, Spike! You woke me up for this shit?" complained Tony. "These bald-headed fuckers look just like you! What are you? Mr. Spike . . . and these are all the little Spikes? Where's Mrs. Spike?" The Marines weren't amused. Spike shook his head and looked at his friends, as though he wanted to direct their attention away from the arrogant airman lying next to him.

"You got that right, Tony!" Spike answered with pride. "These *are* my kids. I raised them from young pups and taught them everything they know. If you're looking for a Mrs. Spike . . . you might as well understand . . . we all married the same lady . . . THE CORPS!"

"Yeah, Spike, educate the flyboy real good!" chimed in one of his comrades. "You want we should jack-him-up?"

"Shut the fuck up, Linowski! What the hell do you know anyway?"

"Easy, sarge. Is this a friend of yours?"

"Yeah, he is . . . kind of. Sometimes Tony got a big mouth . . . he just ain't had the right *motivation*! I would have made a good *shit-hot* Marine out of him!" The four suntanned troopers

A Star of Honor

laughed together with their leader, as he joked in jargon only they could understand.

"Aw, come on, sarge! You gone soft in the brain or something? This pansey could never be a Marine!"

"Okay, you guys. Knock it off!" shouted Spike. "In case you fuckers ain't got on your glasses today, this man is wearing a Silver Star . . . and he didn't get that Purple Heart for cutting himself shaving! Let's have a little respect here!" The other Marines became silent at once. They heeded the stern advice of their sergeant. They began treating Tony with the reverence and respect, a Silver Star winner was entitled, according to the standards they had set for themselves. "Where the hell is Gunney Jackson? He ought to have his head examined, letting you bums run loose in the P.I. (Philippine Islands)! If I would have known you was coming, I would have warned the people downtown to lock up their daughters, and hide their wives!"

"Gunney Jackson bought it, sarge," answered Linowski, his face becoming stiff as if it were chiseled from a block of stone.

"Bought it? When? I can't believe it! How'd it happen?"

"You remember how gunney loved animals, right? Well, the same day you got hit, . . . that's when it happened."

"What the hell's animals got to do with killing gunney, you asshole?"

"Let the man talk, Spike," interrupted Tony.

"Remember he had that little brown monkey he kept for a pet? Well . . . he always carried it in his pack wherever he went. We began chasing a V.C. patrol into the bush, outside the perimeter. Before we realized what was going on, they came at us from all directions. More Viet Cong than I'd ever seen in my entire life! We laid down lots of ground fire and tossed a shitload of grenades, but it just wasn't enough to beat the little fuckers off! Gunney's monkey somehow got out of the pack and ran into a hootch (thatched hut), that sat between them and us. Gunney went berserk and took off after it. He followed it through the

A Star of Honor

door, and that's when the gooks took him out." Sweat poured from Linowski's face, and his terror-stricken eyes were soon filled with tears. "When it was all over . . . we found him. He took so many rounds . . . his body was cut in two. We saw his monkey lying dead next to him. FUCKING gook-bastards! They even killed the goddamned monkey!" Spike stared out the window in disbelief. The news of the death of one of his very best friends, was too much for him.

"I could use a drink." Johnson, the youngest of the group, pulled a flask of whiskey from his back pocket. Garcia, a Mexican-American, and the only hispanic in the group, left the room to find cups. He returned with seven glasses. Johnson poured the whiskey into seven equal portions, handing one to Spike, then to each of the others. They passed one of the filled glasses from man to man, and the last one in line gave it to Tony. One glass stood alone on the night table, to symbolize the sharing of one last drink with a fallen hero. All the glasses were then raised in a toast. "To Gunnary Sergeant, Jeff Jackson!" shouted Spike. "The greatest Marine that ever lived, and my best friend . . . I loved him like a brother! May the bugles honor him with one last tribute, and may his spirit march with us forever!" They drank their toast together, then shattered the glasses, one-by-one against the wall. Tears rolled down Spike's cheeks. Tony could feel the anguish and pain emerging from the hearts of his newly-found brothers, for at that instant, they each shared a feeling of mutual respect.

Spike called Garcia over to his bed, and whispered something in his ear. The Mexican reached under his shirt. From behind the belt holding up his trousers, he pulled out a cumbersome object wrapped in a handkerchief, and handed it to Spike. Spike placed it under his pillow and then shook the hands of his fellow Marines. They all bid him farewell, and slowly filed out the door.

Tony was so consumed with emotion, he couldn't speak. Spike lay back, and rested his head on the pillow. Their minds slowly drifted to "The Nam." Their dreams would soon return them to the sources of each one's personal, unholy passage, through the intricate bowels of hell.

Chapter 14

The Marines were leaving as Samantha came in to check on them. When they passed in the doorway, Garcia grabbed the nurse, taking her into his arms. He pulled her close and whispered, "I'm in love with you, Chiquita!"

"SAVE IT, JERK!" she screamed, as she smashed the tray she was carrying on top of his head. The Mexican never knew what hit him, as he fell to a sitting position on the floor. "Who wants to be next?" shouted Samantha, swinging the tray blindly at the other Marines.

"Cool it, lieutenant!" yelled Linowski, as he bent down to help Garcia to his feet. Still in a state of shock, Garcia threw his arm over Linowski's shoulder. He turned to Samantha and said, "I like my women hot! Next time, baby!" Samantha took another swing at him.

"Next time?! If you ever put your hands on me again, you'll be singing the Marine Hymn as a soprano!" The Marines all laughed at Garcia, as they meandered down the hall.

"Take it easy, Sam," said Tony. "Those guys are just a little

A Star of Honor

on the crazy side."

"I came over here to care for the sick and wounded, not be accosted by idiots with perverted minds!" she answered, rather upset.

"Okay, Sam. Are you here for a reason?"

"Now, Tony, don't you start on me! I had enough of this crap for one day!"

"Well, what is it you need anyway, Sam?" She spied the broken glass on the floor, her eyes confronting the two innocent-looking culprits, trying to avoid the inevitable.

"What the hell happened in here? Did those animals who just left do this? Did they hurt you?"

"Let it be, Sam! It's a long story. Can't you see we're busy? Why don't you come back and bitch at us later, when we have more time. Our dance cards are full right now."

"You two burn me up! I got ten minutes 'till shift change. Damn you two!" She began cleaning up the mess, hoping to be done before Tia signed on to relieve her. Samantha worked quickly, but to her dismay, Tia arrived a few minutes early.

"Hi, good-looking. Hi, Spike. What the . . .? Nope, I'm not even going to ask! Lieutenant, call an orderly to clean up that mess! That's not what the Air Force pays you to do!"

"Yes, ma'am," answered Samantha, leaving the room. Tia shook her head.

"Why don't you give *me* a hard time like you give her, Tony?"

"Well, we'd hate to get the shit beat out of us, that's why!" Tony grinned and Tia hugged him.

"You always make me laugh, Tony, even when I know you've been up to no good! What's wrong with my other baby over there?"

"He had some bad news, mamma-san, but I think he'll get over it."

"Spike, what's wrong?" Spike wouldn't answer. He con-

A Star of Honor

tinued staring out the window, as if entranced by demons from another world.

"Let him be, Tia. I'm serious . . . just leave him alone, okay?"

"Okay, Tony. I'll check on him later. But right now, I have to go sign on this shift so I can legally take care of you bad boys." Before she left, she kissed Spike on the forehead. He never moved from his rigid position. She then kissed Tony in the same manner, and started for the door. An orderly summoned by Samantha, rushed into the room, cleaned up the glass, and hastily left.

"I'll be back later."

"Okay, mamma-san, take care. I got a few things to tell you anyway, so don't stay away too long, all right?"

"Okay, Tony . . . bye!"

"Bye, Tia! Later, baby!"

A tree outside their window rocked in the gusty wind. It screeched against the pane like chalk on a blackboard. Spike became lost deep in thought. He tossed and turned, as best his hulking body would allow. "Tony?" he said, almost in a whisper. "You still here?"

"No, Spike . . . I walked out of here when the light went out. Of course I'm here. Where the hell do you think I would be?"

"Does it ever bother you . . . being a gimp, I mean?" he asked, barely able to push out the words.

"Buddy, I don't believe what that asshole, Jacobson says!" Tony replied, carefully considering the rest of his response before continuing. "I'm positive lying in this bed is only a temporary setback!"

"But, Tony, I was a damn good runner once! I was a champion!"

"I know, buddy, I know. We may have been dealt a shitty hand, but however . . . we still got a chance to cheat the system a little. I don't ever give up! Hey, man! We're G.I.s, we can adapt, right? Ain't you the meanest motherfucker in the corps?" Tony re-

A Star of Honor

plied with a smile. Spike didn't answer. Tony thought he had fallen asleep, so he closed his eyes and tried to block the Marine's morbid words from his mind. He had hoped Tia would soon finish her rounds, and come back to his bedside to comfort him. He was lulled to sleep by the building rocking gently in the wind.

A crash of thunder cracked overhead, as another Pacific storm quickly arrived on the islands. It provoked him, as it lashed out at the hospital. Like an evil dragon, it seemed to drift away with his soul, carrying him back to the terror-filled nightmares in the jungle he tried so desperately to forget. Tony became hopelessly lost in his dream and didn't notice Spike was sitting up. The Marine reached under his pillow, and carefully slid out the object he had hidden there. Gingerly, he unwrapped the handkerchief and let it drop to the floor below. Spike was now holding a blue-steel, automatic pistol in his hand. As he pointed the gun forward, he checked the clip for ammunition. When he was convinced it was loaded, he quietly drew back the slide, cocking the hammer. He switched the safety to the "on" position. He stared off into the night storm, as he took aim at the big oak tree swaying furiously outside the window. Spike looked over at Tony, who was now enduring extreme torment of his own. "Yeah, buddy, you would have made a shit-hot Marine. Gunney Jackson would have liked you, and I liked you too. Take care, flyboy. Keep on fighting! Kick ass and take names!" Tears streamed down his face and steadily dropped onto his pajamas. He raised the gun to his head and moved the safety to the "off" position. He shouted out, "I love you, mom! God, forgive me!" He crossed himself, and a shot rang out through the winding corridors of the hospital.

Like a mighty oak tree, falling unnoticed in a dark forest, the big Marine lay dead. His loves, his fears, his life . . . would be no more.

Chapter 15

The resonant sound of the gunshot was distinct, as its blood-chilling pitch echoed loudly throughout the hospital. It was clearly heard over the constant roar of the howling thunderstorm, which relentlessly pounded the building. Tia feared the worst. She ran as fast as her legs would carry her, in the direction of an obvious premonition of trouble. The door was about to fly off the hinges as she dashed into the room. Orderlies and patients from other areas on the ward crowded outside in the hallway, trying to see the cause of all the commotion. Tia saw Tony propped up in his bed, his face buried in both hands. He appeared to be crying. "Tony! Are you guys all right? Oh my god! What happened!" Tia cautiously approached Spike, quickly examining him for any vital life signs. She found no pulse or heartbeat. After realizing what Spike had done, she sat down on Tony's bed and stared at the bizarre and unbelievable scene before them. Tia turned to Tony, who would not speak, and pressed his head against her breast, as she gently rocked him. She held him for a while and then stepped down from the bed. "Get out of here!" she yelled at the onlookers, who by this time were peering

A Star of Honor

through the entrance of the room. "I have three requests," she said, motioning to one of the orderlies to come forward.

"Yes, ma'am?"

"First, I want you to see that this area is cleared, and that all these patients are sent back to their beds. Second, I want you to call the Security Police and report this incident. Lastly, I want you to close the door and leave us alone for a few minutes."

"Yes, ma'am," he responded, as he herded the curious crowd of walking wounded from the room. The door was closed and Tia sat with Tony. She held his hand and rubbed it softly against her cheek. She kissed him, and they embraced. "I've lost a member of my family tonight, and I don't know why," she whispered, cradling him in her arms. His warm tears blended with hers, as they mourned the painful loss of their friend. Tony attempted to push her away, but she refused to release him. "I know you're angry, but please believe me when I tell you, he would have done this anyway. He never listened to any of us when we tried to help him. I lost one of you, but I swear to God, I won't lose the other. So, whatever you're thinking . . . put it out of your head right now! Understand, airman?" she sobbed. Tia was afraid Tony might attempt the same thing, if given half a chance. Tony again tried pushing her away. He reached down to the pocket on his pajama top and grabbed hold of the medals he was wearing. With one smooth motion, he tore them off and waved them angrily in front of Tia's face.

"I told you, I don't deserve these! Give them to that brave kid over there. He should have them . . . not me!" he shouted, pointing to the bed where Spike was lying.

"But, Tony, you earned the right to wear those medals. They belong to *you*!" Tony's face became taut. His heart pounded wildly within his chest. He felt at any moment, it would burst from rage. He threw the medals across the room, and watched as they hit the wall and came to rest on the floor. The Purple Heart

53

A Star of Honor

landed face down, with the Silver Star falling close beside it. The hero's medals were illuminated by a flash of lightning, which cast a shadow over him as he wept.

"I will always be here for you, Tony, don't you realize that?" Tia whispered in his ear as she tried to calm him. He fell exhausted, into her waiting arms.

"I want to believe that, mamma-san. But at this point . . . I'm very confused."

"I do understand, good-looking. Please put your trust in me . . . and your faith in God."

"I *do* trust you, Tia. I really do. I already had a meeting with God, face to face." He pointed toward the window and looked into the blackness of the night. "Out there. In the jungles of Nam! I swear it was God . . . He came to me! That's why I didn't die out there. That's why I'm here . . . alive now!" Tia gently covered his lips to quiet him, then walked over to Spike's bed. The young Filipino nurse draped a white bedsheet over the body. Before her, she drew the sign of the cross with her hand, as she uttered a farewell prayer for the dead Marine.

"Don't leave me tonight!" Tony begged, clutching the collar of her uniform as she leaned over him.

"I won't. I promise with all my heart. But for now, I must go to the next room to get my equipment. It won't take long." Tia pressed the call button, which brought a responding orderly into the room. He was given instructions to watch Tony as she went to get his medication from the locked drug cabinet in her office. She soon reappeared carrying the morphine he so desperately needed. Tia injected him and proceeded to give one last set of directions to the orderly before sending him away. "As soon as this man is asleep, I want him moved out of this room, is that clear?"

"Yes, ma'am. I'll make the arrangements as soon as possible!"

"Thank you, sergeant."

Tia held Tony close to her, and as he rested peacefully, si-

A Star of Honor

lently prayed for all the agony and pain to quickly pass. She then bent down to retrieve Tony's medals from the floor, dusting them off, as she tried to restore their dignity. For a brief moment, Tia clasped them tightly over her heart, then slowly, but carefully, pinned each of the heroic symbols back on the ripped pocket they were torn from. Deep in her thoughts she knew, this was a night, that would not be forgotten. She hoped as a new morning drew near, it would bring about a much happier day.

Chapter 16

Tony lie on the bed in his new room, quietly reading magazines. Two soft hands covered his eyes, as a female voice rang out, "Guess who?"

"Shit, I don't know. Who the hell is it?"

"Oh, Tony! What's wrong with you today?" asked Tia, climbing up on the bed with him.

"Tia, do you remember when they first brought me in here?"

"If you mean when they brought you into the hospital, Tony, I don't think I could ever forget! Why?"

"Well . . . did I ever mention a guy named Jim Garver?"

"You raved on for several days when they brought you to us. You had many nightmares, just as you do now. I can try to remember all the names you mentioned, but there were so many. Who is Jim Garver?"

"Oh . . . just someone I used to know, that's all. Tia, would you do me a favor? I need you to check the records in the hospital Admissions Office to see if someone by that name was admitted during the last three months, okay?"

A Star of Honor

"Tony, I definitely will not! Unless of course . . . you stop acting so mysterious and tell me what this is all about!"

"Okay, you win! You dragged it out of me. Jim was a guy I went through basic training with. We also went through technical training school at Sheppard together. That's when the Air Force made grease monkeys out of us!" he said, smiling.

"But why is he so important, good-looking?"

"Well, Tia, I have something that belongs to him, and I would like to return it. That's all there is to it!"

"Show it to me, and I'll determine if this is worth my time or not!"

"I don't have it here, Tia. It's in a small, green canvas bag. They locked it up in the hospital safe with the rest of my stuff. Would you be a sweet, little brown Filipino baby, and go get it for me?"

"Well . . . if it's that important to you, I'll fetch it for you. I'll have to obtain a release form for you to sign, then I can get access to your belongings." With her curiosity stimulated, Tia quickly departed to find a signature form. She hoped this would be a positive step in the right direction, to help clear up the mystery that seemed to weigh heavy on Tony's mind. While doing so, she checked the records in the Admissions Office. A friend, who was also a captain, owed her a favor she was now determined to collect. He allowed her to look through the confidential admissions files, however, no records on a Jim Garver could be found. The captain also let her take the small canvas bag from the safe, without the required form. "Now, Tia, if you breathe a word of this to anyone . . . it's my butt!"

"Okay, Al! It's no sweat! Thanks for being so sweet!"

"Say, Tia, what are my chances of taking you out to dinner?"

"Sorry, Al. No chances at all!"

"Oh, well," he replied, in a disappointed tone. "You can't blame a guy for trying!"

"Tia hurried back to Tony's room with the article he re-

A Star of Honor

quested. She wanted to peek inside, but restrained herself, as she handed it to him. Tony thanked her, and put the bag under his pillow. He closed his eyes, giving her the impression he was going to sleep. "Oh, no you don't! I went through a lot of trouble for you . . . now *tell me*!"

"Tell you what?" teased Tony.

"What the hell is in the bag!"

"Okay, mamma-san, you win again!" He removed the bag from under his pillow and laid it on his lap. Tia climbed up on the bed and made herself comfortable. "Hmmm . . . nice legs, mamma-san."

"Now cut that out, smart-ass!" she protested, as she adjusted her dress back down over her knees. "Now, talk!"

Tony untied the drawstring, pulling back the pleated material. He removed a tattered black and white photograph. The picture was covered with mildew and appeared to have been stained with blood. He handed it to Tia, and reached into the bag once again. He took out a gold wedding band, examined it, and gave that to her as well. Cautiously, Tony's hand returned to the canvas version of Pandora's Box, this time retrieving a gold Bulova watch. Tia held the watch up to the light, and silently read the inscription on the back. 'To my husband, Jim. Although our married life together has been short, my love for you is forever. First Wedding Anniversary, 6-21-68, Love always, Helen.'

"What are these things, Tony?"

"He asked me to watch over this stuff for him, in case he didn't make it. I promised him I would."

"What do you mean, Tony?"

"It's very tough to explain, Tia."

"You mean . . . he didn't make it, Tony? Is that why you have his things?"

"I don't know, damnit!" he snapped. "I just don't know what happened to him!"

A Star of Honor

"Tony, does this have anything to do with your medals?"

"I really don't know, mamma-san, I just can't be sure. I want to see that Helen, his wife, gets these things. That's all, Tia. You know I never make a promise I can't keep. I promised him, and now comes my time to keep that promise. Do you understand?" Tia nodded her head and looked into Tony's deeply penetrating brown eyes. She stroked his black hair with her hand.

"You act like such a damn tough-guy all the time, never caring for anyone but yourself. Yet, you're so concerned about a photo, a ring, and a watch. All together, these things wouldn't bring fifty dollars on the black market. Okay, tough-guy! I'll help you find your answers. I'll start researching Air Force records tomorrow, but you have to promise me something."

"And what might that be, mamma-san?"

"Tony, I want to know everything about you, good and bad included. I need to understand what causes all the terror you endure each and every night."

"And what will that prove, Tia?"

"Perhaps nothing, Tony. But I can't pray for God to help you if I don't know what to ask for."

"Nice try, baby! I'm finished talking about it now. I'm very tired. I need some sleep."

Tia helped him return the items to the bag. They looked at the photograph together for a brief moment. It was a picture of a young couple in wedding attire. They were no more than children, their lives torn apart by a country's call to duty. Written in ink on the back of the photo were the words: 'Our Wedding Day, 6-21-67. I miss you, Jim . . . please come home soon! Your loving wife, Helen.' Tia climbed down from the bed and promised to return later. "I must now do some of the work the Air Force is paying me good money for! I'll lock that up for you, okay?"

"No, I'll keep it here with me. I have a lot to think about, mamma-san."

"All right, Tony, as you wish. Don't stay up too late, okay?"

A Star of Honor

"Okay, mommy," he mused.

Tia kissed him and returned to her busy duties on the ward. Tony stared at the photograph again. Tears rolled down his cheeks and dripped onto the blood-stained picture. "Don't worry," he said. "Wherever she is, buddy, I'll see that she gets your personal effects. I always keep a promise!" Tony put the bag back under his pillow. He clutched the photograph in his hand and continued, "After all, if you can't trust a buddy, who can you trust?" He closed his eyes and prayed. He asked for Him to make possible, the keeping of a sacred vow, which he whispered to a buddy in the jungle as they both had lain but one step away from the icy claws of death.

Chapter 17

Tony spent most of the night lost in thought about the fate of Jim Garver. Tia quietly entered the room, going unnoticed as she watched him. 'My poor baby. He must have ignored my orders and stayed up all night.' "Hi, Tony! What's up?"

"Jesus Christ, lady! Don't ever do that again!"

"Do what, good-looking?"

"Don't ever sneak up on me like that! You scared the shit out of me!"

"My goodness, Tony! What's your problem *today*? Didn't you sleep well last night?"

"Actually, no, mamma-san. I didn't do too well in the sleep department."

"What's on your mind, honey? Why didn't you rest?"

"Don't trouble yourself with it, okay? What you really need to think about is what will happen to you if you ever sneak up on me again!"

"Oh? Are we going into our tough, little boy act again?"

"All right, Tia. You win this time. But next time, I'll . . ."

A Star of Honor

"You'll what, Tony?"

"I'll spank your little brown butt, that's what!"

"Ha! That'll be the day! I don't think you could punch your way out of a wet paper bag with brass knuckles!"

"Oh, is that so?" he said, tightly grasping her wrists. Even though he wasn't able to move his legs, Tia could feel the enormous strength in Tony's arms and upper body.

"Let me go!" she protested, pretending to put up a struggle.

"Never, mamma-san!" He pulled her onto the bed, almost on top of him.

"I said, let go!"

"Why, baby? Who says so?"

"I say so! I'm a captain, and you're an airman, and because . . . I'm giving you an order and I . . . I . . ." She was stopped in mid-conversation as he pressed his lips to hers and held her close. She accepted his inviting advance, and fell victim to the persistence of his Italian charm. She returned the kiss with one equally as passionate, as she gently massaged his back. Then, just as suddenly as they had come together, she pushed away. "No, Tony, stop! This isn't right and we must stop now!"

"Stop? Why, mamma-san? Something wrong with the way I kiss?"

"Please stop," she sobbed.

"Oh, I get it! You don't want to be stuck with a cripple all your life, right?"

"Now, look at me, Tony. I shouldn't be telling you this, but now I suppose I have to. Falling in love with a handsome devil like you would be so easy for me to do. At times I feel it's very possible. You being a cripple never entered my mind. It wouldn't make any difference to me, anyway. But however, I'm afraid that one . . . or both of us, would get hurt in the end. That would just be too much for me to bear. Besides, we could lose this wonderful relationship which took so long for us to find, and I'm afraid that would be a tragedy."

A Star of Honor

"I'm sorry, Tia. I know you're right. I guess we just got carried away. What we have is very special. Let's not fuck it up by falling in love."

"Tony, do you mean that?"

"Yes, ma'am, I surely do! Tia? Would you mind if I loved you for the wonderful woman you are, without being *in* love with you?"

"Of course not, good-looking. I wouldn't want it any other way! But you need to know of course, I also love you. You try so hard to be a vicious tiger, and you *can* be when you have to. But, I know under it all, you're really a sweet little pussycat."

"What?!"

"But I promise. I won't tell a soul. It's just between us."

"For sure, baby?"

"Really, for sure, good-looking." Their lips met once again, and they found in each other a close, intimate relationship neither had ever known before. "I must leave now, Tony. I need to go to my home off base and get a little sleep. I'll be back to visit around noon. I'll have a surprise for you then."

"What kind of surprise, sweet thing?"

"Well, if I told you, it would be ruined, so there!"

"Okay, kill-joy. Be that way!"

"Yes, my little spoiled baby. I will!"

"Well, don't take all day getting back, okay, mamma-san."

"All right, good-looking. This time it's you who wins! Let me go and freshen up at home so I can get out of this white monkey-suit! I'll be back as soon as I can."

"You're so good to me, Tia. I really don't deserve it."

"Oh, Tony, stop it. Now be a good little boy until I get back, okay?"

"Yes, ma'am," he snapped.

"Now rest a little bit for me, Tony. That's an order from your nurse, understand?"

"All right, already! The quicker you go . . . the quicker I get

A Star of Honor

my surprise when you get back! Mamma-san?"
"Yes?"
"I love you, 'ya know?"
"I know that, tough-guy! Now, I'm really leaving, okay?"
"Okay, Tia, I'll be waiting for you."

She blew him a kiss as she walked to the door. He watched as she disappeared slowly down the long hallway. As Tony lie on his pillow, he daydreamed about this special lady in his life. He thought to himself, 'That's an O.K. chick . . . for a goddamned officer!' He watched through his window, as the fluffy white clouds drifted lazily across the blue sky. He hoped he could find happiness in his new relationship. He felt at that moment, sharing all his deep, innermost secrets with her, would definitely be a wonderful idea.

Chapter 18

The morning hours became noon, and noon turned to one o'clock. Tony grew more frustrated with each passing minute, wondering what could have happened to Tia. 'I bet she went to sleep and forgot all about me. I'll smack her butt when she does get here!' His silent thoughts were soon replaced by the cheerful sounds of Tia's voice.

"Hi, good-looking. I'm back! Did you miss me?"

"Where the hell have you been? You're late! I figured you weren't coming."

"Oh, Tony. I wouldn't have missed this for the world!"

"Missed what, mamma-san?"

"Why . . . the surprise I have for you, tough-guy, that's what!"

"Surprise? Well . . . I really hadn't thought about it."

"Sorry I'm late, but I had to borrow my brother's jeep. I also brought some people here for you to meet." She called out a few words in her native Tagalog language. The door opened, and two very young, brown-skinned Filipino girls entered. They each

A Star of Honor

wore a brightly colored, hand-sewn cotton dress and brown sandals, which highlighted their pink polished toenails. Both girls had long, flowing coal black hair that hung almost to their waists.

"Are they yours?"

"No, silly! They're my sisters. This is Lisa, who is twelve, and Lett, who is nine." The girls politely bowed their heads in Tony's direction, smiling sweetly. They stared at him for a little while and finally, Lisa spoke.

"Are you my sister's friend? Are you the hero?"

"Okay, girls! Enough questions, please!" ordered Tia. "Now wait over there while I get Tony ready." The girls promptly obeyed, but went outside to pass the time.

"What is this, Tia? Kiddie day or something?"

"This is my surprise for you, good-looking!"

"You brought me a couple of kids for a surprise? What kind of shit is this?"

"They agreed to chaperon us. I also brought you these . . ." She emptied a brown paper bag on the bed. A light blue, embroidered shirt and a pair of white slacks fell out in front of him. "I hope they fit. I had to do some guessing on the sizes."

"What's this all about?"

"Okay, Tony, I suppose I've kept you in the dark long enough. I've got the whole weekend off, and we're going to take you to the mountains in the city of Baguio. Have you ever been there?"

"Nope, I can't say I have. But I'm not going anywhere with anybody! A lot of fun that would be for you and those girls out there . . . dragging a cripple around all over the country. I don't want all the people staring at me with pity. I don't think I could stand much of that, baby."

"Oh stop your griping, tough-guy. You need to get a change of scenery anyway, so you *will* be going with us on this trip. We'll stay in my uncle's cabin, and we'll all have a wonderful time!"

A Star of Honor

"Tia, why are you doing this?"

"Because I want to! Now let's get you dressed, okay? We have a long drive ahead of us and the road is hot this time of day." Tony stopped his protesting long enough for Tia to slip him out of his pajamas.

"You're pretty good at this, lady!"

"Lots of practice. Now help me a little by closing your big trap!" Tony understood the not-so-subtle hint, and stayed quiet as Tia helped him dress for the outing. When he was ready, she called her sisters to join them. In they strolled pushing a chrome wheelchair. "All right now, good-looking, just be still while we help you into this chair."

The three sisters worked together as they gently lifted Tony into the chair. When he was in place, they slowly moved him out the door and down the long hospital corridor. He was rolled past the big carved oak doors of the chapel and out into the afternoon warmth of the sunny courtyard. They followed a tree-shaded, cobblestone path leading to the street. The girls, and a complaining Tony, stopped at the curb where a freshly waxed jeep was waiting. "This is called a jeepney, in the Philippines. It will be our transportation, so don't say a word . . . relax, and leave the rest of the traveling to us!"

"Who's driving this wreck? You, Tia?"

"I told you to be quiet, Tony! And yes, I will be driving. Any objections?"

"Nope. Press on."

Tony was lifted from the chair and deposited into the passenger side of the jeep. Tia placed the rest of his things on the floor in the rear. The girls got in the back, as Tia slid her sleek, blue-jeaned figure into the driver's seat. Making a minor adjustment to the mirror, she turned the slightly tarnished key in the ignition. The engine started with a loud backfire, forcing a billow of black smoke from the tailpipe. Tia tugged on the gearshift, while operating the clutch. Off they chugged, toward the main

A Star of Honor

gate of the base. Passing in front of the guard shack, they entered the strange and noisy carnival-like atmosphere of the bustling city of Angeles. Weaving through the traffic of honking jeeps and motorcycles, their weekend adventure began.

Chapter 19

The intense heat of the afternoon sun soon took its toll on the jeep's occupants. Tia stopped by the side of the road seeking shade from a nearby tree for her passengers. "Why are we stopping?" Tony asked.

"We need to get some refreshments and put up the canvas top. Are you feeling any pain?"

"No, mamma-san, I'm hanging in there. I am a bit thirsty though."

"So are we, Tia!" came two voices in protest from the backseat.

"Okay, troops, we're saved! I brought some soda-pop along. Lisa, you give everyone a cold drink, and Lett . . . you can help me put the roof back on this Filipino Cadillac!" Tia's younger helpers were of great assistance, as one reached into the icechest to retrieve the soft drinks, and the other began unrolling the vehicle's cover.

After the travelers quenched their thirsts, and all was secured, they were off again. The picturesque scenery of the rice

A Star of Honor

paddies along the way, with people feverishly laboring in them, were reminiscent to Tony of Vietnam. His mind wandered back to the memories constantly haunting him. The girls sang school songs, and the jeep's engine sputtered, trying its best to carry them. The roads became curved and narrow; the presence of villages being few and far between. The elevations grew higher, and the dry, dusty highway was soon garnished with a colorful, floral landscape. Pine trees by the hundreds, proudly displayed their magnificent branches of dark emerald green. "Look, Tony! Around the next bend is one of my favorite places." Tony's attention was snatched away from thoughts of his private war by the sweetness of Tia's voice. "Are you sleeping, good-looking?"

"No, Tia. I'm okay," came a dazed reply. "What is it you wanted to show me, mamma-san?"

"Here it is now, Tony!" she answered, as she eased the vehicle to a squealing, but gentle stop. Tony was amazed at the sight.

"Mamma-mia, this is something else!" he exclaimed, in a mimicked Italian accent. Together, they all focused on the splendor of majestic waterfalls, cascading their cool, crystal clear waters downward over the lush, fertile valley below.

"My father used to stop at this place with me on our way to my uncle's cabin when I was a very little girl. He used to tell me it was the playground of the angels. He made me believe if you wished for something here, the saints would grant it."

"That's a bunch of bullshit, Tia! Just a fairytale . . . that's all!"

"That's your problem, Tony! You've got to learn to follow your dreams, to fulfill your destiny. Perhaps if you believed in just one little fairytale, you might find some of the happiness denied you all your life. I never grew up in the streets of New York, like you did, so I don't really understand your bitterness. But I do know you've carried it deep inside for a very long time. I'm convinced it started even before you were sent to Vietnam."

"Goddamnit, Tia! You think you know everything, don't you?"

A Star of Honor

"Nope, not everything. But . . . I do know *you*! Under that rough exterior beats the heart of a pretty sweet guy." Tony became silent, listening intently to the rest of Tia's lecture. "I grew up in a village comprised of very poor people. My parents taught me to work hard for everything. Although we went without many items, we still were able to find happiness in our home. My family had nothing, but we always kept sacred in our hearts the one gift God gave to us for free . . . love. Do you understand what I'm trying to say, Tony?"

"I think so, mamma-san. You do seem to be committed to that cause. You always find a little bit of love to share with everyone, no matter how shitty your day has been. It's just too difficult for me, Tia. It's so damned hard to find love and beauty in a world where I saw children, once as beautiful as your sisters, with their throats cut . . . lying on bamboo beds in pools of their own blood. Next to them, their dead parents, and little dolls made of straw." Tia, unable to hold back her tears, took his hand.

"Try to put that ugliness behind you, Tony," she said softly. "Let's all make a wish on the falls. We'll ask the saints to grant peace, love and happiness, to all of God's little children . . . wherever they might be."

"I like that, Tia. Thank you. That's one wish that's not bullshit. Let's do it!"

The girls gathered around Tony as he sat propped up in his seat. As they all tightly held hands, their gazes shifted to the continuous liquid downpour which plunged endlessly onto the rocks, as it had unaltered, for five-hundred years. Lisa handed Tia a lavender orchid she picked from where it grew wild among the foliage. They each pulled a petal from the beautiful flower, and tossed it into the spray of the mighty torrent, as they meditated in silence.

Shortly thereafter, Tia abruptly ordered everyone into the jeep. When all were ready to proceed on the journey, she backed it out slowly onto the road and pressed on. She daydreamed

A Star of Honor

about her childhood, and of the love she remembered sharing with her family. She thought perhaps her father was right about wishing on the falls, and strongly maintained her faith that their humble requests would be granted. Tia prayed she and her sisters might be allowed to present sopme of that same love and hope found in their lives, to Tony Magnacavello, street kid from New York.

Chapter 20

Soon their ascent into the mountain village would be complete. Temperatures became cooler, as Tony and the girls neared the city of Baguio with great anticipation. "The air is so clean and refreshing up here," Tony said, taking a deep breath. "Why is it so foggy though? Are we expecting rain?"

"That's not fog, good-looking! We're so high up on this mountain, that we're in the middle of a cloud formation. Isn't it beautiful?"

"Sure got that fucking rat-trap hospital beat. I'm glad you talked me into this, mamma-san."

"First of all, mister, my hospital is not a rat-trap! And secondly, I hope you'll be happy here. I'm sure we'll all have fun, so quit complaining, all right?"

"And why ain't it a rat-trap?"

"You never saw any rats on my ward, wise-guy!"

"Oh yeah? How can you be so sure of that, mamma-san?"

"Well, partly because Dr. Jacobson eats them for dinner!"

"Are you putting me on, baby?"

A Star of Honor

"Of course I am, silly . . . I'm just being ugly. I'm sorry. Let's not discuss that fool anymore. We don't want to ruin our weekend."

"Okay, baby, you got my vote on that. But I'll bet he *does* eat rats!" They all laughed at Tony's remark as the overcrowded jeep inched its way through the busy market place, rolling past throngs of shopping villagers.

"It won't be long now, troops!"

"That's good, mamma-san. This trip has left me in boo-koo pain!"

"Oh my god! Tony, do you hurt badly?"

"Yeah, baby, I guess I do."

"Hang on, honey, we're almost there!"

"Okay, mamma-san, but hurry!"

They drove through a dense forest of spruce trees, while closing in on the cabin which was to be their vacation retreat. Tia brought them as near to the brown log building as they could possibly get. "Are we here yet, sister?" asked a sleepy-eyed Lisa.

"Yes, we are. Here is the key to the cabin. Open it quickly and get the chair!" Lisa climbed down from the jeep and grabbed the key. Lett then joined her, as they opened the lock, and pushed hard on the small, weather-beaten door. They entered as fast as they could, and soon reappeared in the doorway, pushing a vintage World War II wheelchair.

"Wow! Now this is what I call service!" exclaimed Tony.

"Glad you like this hotel, good-looking. That chair was used by my uncle after his boating accident at Subic Bay, in 1959. He had two broken legs and stayed a long time at this place to ensure himself a restful recovery. He even had a ramp built to make moving about the grounds much easier for him." Tia slipped out from behind the steering wheel and walked to the steps. She attacked a wooden ramp to the front porch and pushed the chair close to where Tony was sitting. The sisters all went into action once again, expeditiously moving Tony. They carefully picked

A Star of Honor

him up, and gingerly set the crippled airman into the chair. They wheeled him up the ramp, over the porch, and into the house with a minimum of discomfort.

"Sorry I'm such a pain in the ass, ladies."

"We don't want to hear any more of that nonsense!" said Tia. "We *will* have a good time! Do you understand, buster? Try to keep an open mind!"

"Yes, ma'am. When's supper?"

"Well, that's a good sign . . . being hungry, I mean. Food will be coming soon. I'll give you a shot if you hurt really bad."

"How did you get drugs out of the hospital anyway, Tia?"

"I hid them in my bra, *okay*?"

"Goddamnit, woman! I asked a simple question, and got a smart-ass answer in return!"

"Oh, Tony, give me a break! I brought the medicine for my patient. Now let your mouth rest." He clutched at her blouse, the pain clearly visible on his grimacing face.

"It hurts bad, mamma-san. Shoot me up! I need it bad!"

"Lisa! Get my black-zippered bag . . . hurry! Now take it easy, good-looking. Help's on the way!" The puzzled girl did exactly as she was told, and watched with curiosity as an injection was prepared. "You two leave now and find something else to do, okay?" The girls rushed to get outside, as she jabbed Tony's hip with the needle. She held him tightly in her arms, as the morphine rapidly subdued his pain. "Feeling better now, good-looking?"

"Much better, mamma-san. That shit really works fast. Either I'm getting high or . . . you're a mighty fine looking woman!"

"Okay, wise-guy . . . I've had enough of this. We need to get our things unpacked so I can show you this very beautiful part of my country."

"Hell girl, you sure got serious on me in a big hurry! Thought we were here to have fun!"

A Star of Honor

"That's right, Tony, and we will have fun. But I'm in charge here *and* the travel director! The kind of fun you have in mind, you can find in a three-piso-per-woman bar . . . not on my tour, understand?"

"Yes, ma'am. Sorry about that!"

Tia called the girls back in to help prepare supper. They moved the supplies from the jeep to the small, but adequate kitchen. All the bags were tossed into the two small bedrooms they would now call home. "Were you ever a Boy Scout?"

"Yes, why do you ask?"

"It gets pretty cold up here at night, so would you mind building us a fire in the fireplace?"

"Sure, baby, no sweat! I don't even need matches! I'm an expert at this kind of stuff!"

"Okay, but try not to burn down the house!"

"Very funny!" he said, as he wheeled himself over to the gray brick fireplace. "Now they ain't got no respect for Boy Scouts either," he mumbled, making sure he was far enough away from Tia so he wouldn't be overheard.

As the sun slowly began to set behind the mountain, the sky became a mass of red and yellow streaks. Tia was busy planning the evening meal, as Lisa and Lett cleaned and chopped vegetables. Tony sat swearing in the wheelchair, unable to start the fire. However, throughout it all, they still managed to savor peace and contentment, as they shared the joys associated with the unknown pleasures of each other's company.

Chapter 21

Tia asked the girls to set the table for supper. She cooked a delightful meal of stir-fried vegetables over rice. The entree was a Filipino specialty called Chicken Fork Adobo. The girls drank canned soda, while Tony and Tia shared a large bottle of San Miguel. Tia shut the cabin lights off, as Tony lit two candles placed near the center of the table. To create a more romantic atmosphere, she turned on her portable radio, tuning it to a station that played only easy-listening music. Tony wanted rock 'n roll, and made that fact readily known.

"What is this? More chicken stuff?"

"So, you don't like my cooking, huh?"

"No! I love this shit, Tia! Can I send the recipe to my mother?"

"Sure, Tony. I'll write it down and you can send it to her . . . oh, I get it! You were just putting me on!"

"Yeah, mamma-san . . . I was. But, however . . . this is some outstanding chow! You really are a great cook," he smiled, munching away at his meal. "I'm glad you didn't insist on me

A Star of Honor

saying grace. My mother always made me say grace at the table when the family was home for the holidays. I absolutely hated it, but always did it. She was always proud of me. I never could figure that one out."

"Were you her youngest, Tony?"

"Yeah. Youngest and dumbest, I guess."

"Dumbest? Why would you say that?"

"Cause I went to Vietnam and got my ass blown off, that's why. And for what? I remember going home on leave, back to Queens in 1968. I was so proud of my uniform and what it stood for. I wore it to show everyone we were doing some good over there. To get to my neighborhood, I had to pass through the Port Authority Bus Terminal. I knew I would have to take a subway as well. When I stepped off the bus and entered the lobby a hippie girl with long hair and beads put a flower in my pocket."

"That was sweet, Tony!"

"Yes, that one was. She was only preaching of peace and love. They call that kind flower children. When I thought all was going well, then came the shit! A chick who was walking with a couple of tough-looking freaks, approached me. I tried to ignore her, but couldn't. She spit on my uniform and called me a baby killer! Can you imagine?! People from the same USA I put my life on the line for, treating me like a pile of dogshit!"

"Yes, I'm sure, baby, an experience like that would make anyone bitter. No, I believe hateful is a better word. But you went back and kept right on doing what you were doing . . . why?"

"Because, mamma-san, I really thought us being there would make the difference between communism and democracy for a country who needed our help."

"Tony, did you really believe that?"

"Well, yes . . . I did at first. But I began to lose faith when I saw what was going on at home . . . chanting and burning American flags in the streets. I became very frustrated and confused. I never wore my uniform home again."

A Star of Honor

"You told me you were proud of that uniform! Why did you stop wearing it?"

"Because, goddamnit! It was just too fucking risky."

"Risky? What do you mean?"

"I spent all that time dodging bullets and rocket attacks. I always stayed dirty and sweaty, never knowing if I would live one day, or die the next! Wouldn't it have been just fucking grand to endure all that crap on a daily basis, only to get killed in my own hometown by Americans? All for wearing a military uniform, and doing the job our country sent us there to do in the first place?"

"Okay, baby, try to calm down! I guess I was wrong to put you on the spot like that. Sorry. After all, I'm a G.I. too!"

"No sweat, mamma-san! Say . . . we got any desert?"

"Yes, we do. Lisa baked us a cake."

"I hope you like it, Tony," said Lisa proudly.

"Well, I know I will, baby-san! Especially since you worked so hard on it." Lisa smiled at Tony and handed him a carved wooden plate heaped with chocolate cake. He winked at her and began devouring it, leaving only crumbs behind.

"Tony?"

"Yes, Tia, what is it, mamma-san?"

"I found that information for you about Jim Garver."

"What?! Why didn't you tell me sooner?"

"I think the time is right now, Tony."

"So tell me, goddamnit!"

"All right! If you'll be quiet, I will! The records indicate an airman by that name was brought in with very severe stomach wounds."

"Yes! That's him!" screamed Tony. "Where is he?"

"Well, as far as I can tell, good-looking, he went to Japan when you were brought to the Philippines. But he was shipped home already."

"Did it say he was alive?"

"I don't know. We'll just have to research this a bit further."

A Star of Honor

"Yeah, I guess so. But I really need to find out!"

"I understand, Tony . . . and I promised you I would help."

"Thanks, Tia. You're a real special lady."

"And you're very welcome, kind sir. Now, wipe that cake off your face and get ready for bed!"

"Yes, ma'am! On my way!"

Tia cleared the table as the girls readied the sink for washing dishes. Tony rolled the wheelchair into the living room, stopping in front of the fireplace. He stared into the crackling fire, remembering his friend, Jim Garver. He wondered if the ordeal they shared together in the jungle had been for real, or only a cruel hoax conjured up in his mind by too many shots of morphine.

Chapter 22

While her sisters were getting ready for bed, Tia joined Tony in front of the fireplace. Still wearing the jeans and apron she had on earlier, she sat down on a woven straw mat on the floor next to his chair, and leaned on a large embroidered throw pillow with a blue silk covering, leaving her in a relaxed state. The burning firewood crackled and popped as a result of her stirring it with a long brass poker. "I love it when it does that."

"Does what, mamma-san?"

"When it makes that crackling sound. The fire is very romantic. I could sit and watch it for hours."

"Me too, baby. I've been fascinated with fire ever since I was a boy."

"Oh, Tony, when did you ever really have time to be a boy?"

"You know, Tia . . . that's really an interesting question."

"Would you like me to pour you a cold glass of beer, good-looking?"

"Sure, baby, I'll split a bottle with you." She poured two glasses of San Miguel and watched as the foam spilled over,

A Star of Honor

slightly running down one and into the small bamboo tray it was standing in.

"I guess I make a pretty poor hostess, huh?"

"You're a great hostess, Tia. Besides, you look very beautiful by firelight."

"Oh, Tony . . . you're such a wonderful liar! But I love it, thank you."

"I've been admiring all those beautiful knives on the walls in the glass cases. Who owns them?"

"They belong to many generations of my family. My father and grandfather were the most avid collectors. The ones over the hearth were my grandfather's favorites." She opened a small wicker cabinet and removed a pouch wrapped in a leather binding, tied with a reed. "These belonged to my father, as they did his father. They're Filipino throwing knoves. This set is almost one hundred years old. The knives are superbly balanced, and when thrown, will penetrate even the hardest of woods."

"I can't believe the craftsmanship of this metal. I bet your family is very proud of them."

"Yes, very proud. In my family, we had a custom which was brought from the Province we lived in. If these knives were to be given by their rightful owner to someone special in his or her life, they would bring luck to both the giver and the receiver. My father gave them to me, and I now present them to you."

"Tia, I just couldn't accept these, honey. They've been in your family for a hundred years!"

"My father would have liked you, Tony. Please do me the honor of accepting them from the whole Ramos family. It means so very much to me."

"I just don't know what to say!"

"Don't say anything, Tony . . . just keep them, okay?"

"I'll always treasure them," he sighed, overcome with emotion. Tony re-wrapped the knives and kept them by his side in the wheelchair. Lisa and Lett soon joined them, wearing colorful

A Star of Honor

nightgowns, walking in their barefeet. They carried marshmallows and several bamboo skewers.

"Is this what American kids do, Tony?" asked Lett.

"That depends, baby-san. What are *you* going to do with them?"

"We read in a magazine American children like to roast them and eat them. Is that true?" asked Lisa.

"Well . . . yes it is, girls! But do you really think you'll like them?"

"Well, we don't know . . . but we'll try!" came the reply. Tia slipped off to the shower room, as Tony helped the girls roast marshmallows. Soon afterwards, she returned wearing a blue silk nightgown, which flowed with the breeze as she strolled into the room. Her long black hair shimmered in the soft flickering shadows. Flames from the pine-scented logs danced playfully within the walls of their brick enclosure.

"Well, girls," Tia said softly. "It's time for you to go to bed."

"Oh sister, do we have to?"

"Say good-night to Tony and go now, all right?"

"All right . . ." they said, in a sad tone of voice. Lisa and Lett each kissed Tony and gave him a big hug. "Good-night, Tony! We liked the marshmallows, but we still don't understand why American kids do that!" They both giggled as they shut the door behind them.

"Good-night, girls!" said Tia sternly.

"Well, alone at last, mamma-san!"

"Time for you to go to bed too, good-looking. We've got lots to do tomorrow!"

"Aw, sister, do I have to?" he joked.

"That's correct, buddy! So let's get moving, airman!" Tia rolled his chair into the shower room and helped him out of his clothes. She gave Tony a sponge bath and gently dried him. She helped put on his pajamas, then wheeled him into the bedroom assigned to him for the weekend. "I just want to sit here for a

83

A Star of Honor

while and enjoy the peace and quiet. I think I can manage myself into the bed later, okay, Tia?"

"Okay, good-looking, but if you need anything . . . please call."

"All right, mamma-san. Good-night, ma'am."

"Good-night, Tony. Sweet dreams, tough-guy."

She kissed him, then left to join her sisters, who were already deep in slumber on their big soft bed. Tony sat in the wheelchair, admiring his newly acquired throwing knives. His eyes closed for a bit and he relaxed, swayed to sleep and soothed by the serenade of crickets chirping their haunting melodies in the cool midnight breezes.

Chapter 23

It wasn't long before Tony was having severe pain. He called for Tia. She knew exactly what the problem was, and came running with the morphine. She administered the injection, and at his request, decided to let him sit in the chair for as long as he wanted. Tia returned to her room and Tony nodded off.

All was quiet, as several tranquil hours drifted by. Suddenly, everyone was awakened by a banging outside at the front of the cabin. Still in a daze, Tony listened as Tia opened her bedroom door, shuffling in her slippers across the floor. "Who is it?"

"Telegram, ma'am."

"Slide it under the door, please."

"Sorry, ma'am . . . you must sign for it."

"Oh, very well. Just one moment please." She hastily tied the sash of a green satin robe and unbolted the heavy wooden door. At that moment, she was pushed out of the way by a strong force on the other side.

She realized too late, she had been deceived. Two unshaven, Filipino men in dirty clothes, came crashing through. "Get out of here!" she screamed. One of the men tried to grab her, as she fought to push him back. She was soon overpowered as her head slammed into the wall, knocking her unconscious as she fell to the floor. Tony wheeled his chair to the bedroom doorway just in time to witness the ugly scene unfolding. Still under the influence of the morphine, and lost in a state of euphoria, everything seemed partly dangerous and partly funny. One of the men was tying up the fallen nurse, as the other began filling a sack with things he intended to steal. Lisa and Lett ran into the room to see what was the matter. They were grabbed by the man filling the sack, as he dropped it to the floor.

"Well, look at this! We found something else to do tonight!"

"Let us go!" screamed Lisa.

"Come here!" he snorted. "We'll make you pretty girls into grown-up women tonight!" The other man, now finished binding Tia, laughed in agreement.

"Yes, pretty girls . . . we'll show you a very good time! Don't fight us, and we won't have to hurt you." Tony wheeled into the room making noise trying to divert the men's attention from the struggling girls.

"Get away from them, you goddamn scumbags!"

"What's this? A cripple in a wheelchair . . . and he's threatening us!" answered one of the perpetrators. They laughed and started walking in his direction. One of them broke off the leg from a chair, with every intention of using it as a club. "No witnesses, cripple-boy. Tonight you'll watch us make two women out of these girls, and then we'll have to kill you. With our records, we can't afford to be identified by anyone."

"Hell you say!" screamed Tony, almost laughing from the drugs in his system. Tia became semi-conscious and rolled over. She slipped one hand partially free and grabbed one of the strangers by the ankle. He fell, and his cohort kicked her arm. Tony reached into the leather pouch by his side and pulled one of the

A Star of Honor

throwing knives. "Hey, you little brown piece of shit! Why don't you kick me, asshole!" he taunted. The man who kicked Tia now faced Tony, swinging the broken chair leg.

"This is your time to die!" he answered. Tony drew back one arm above his head, and threw the knife with all the strength he could muster. It flew like a silver guided missile, across the firelit room.

"Eat this steel . . . you fucker!" Tony screamed, as the precision-tempered blade found its mark, lodging in the shoulder of his tormentor, knocking him off his feet. The other man, seeing what happened, scurried out the door, fleeing into the night.

During the scuffle, Lisa escaped to the kitchen and returned with a skillet. She hit the wounded Filipino on the head, as Lett beat him with the chair leg he'd intended to use on Tony. "That's it, girls! Kick his ass!" grinned the excited airman. He wheeled his chair over to Tia, who was trying to sit up. "Are you hurt, baby?"

"No . . . I think I'll live, good-looking. I'm very ashamed of myself. I did a very stupid thing by opening the door."

"You made a mistake, so what? We handled it . . . we *all* handled it together! You're the toughest gals I ever met!" He reached down, cutting the rest of the bindings from Tia's wrists. Holding on to the wheelchair and Tony, she slowly stood up. A small cut was visible above her left eyebrow.

"Run and fetch the village police, girls!" Tia ordered, giving them a knife to carry for protection. "If the other one returns, use this, okay?"

"Okay!" they said, running out the door. Tony made Tia sit in a chair while he wheeled himself to the other room for the first aid kit. After retrieving it, along with a pan of soap and water, he worked on Tia's cut.

"I'm fine, Tony. Leave me alone!"

"Shut up, mamma-san! My turn to take care of you!" he snapped. He cleaned and dressed her wound. Tia cried and hug-

A Star of Honor

ged him.

"We owe you our lives, Tony."

"You owe me nothing, baby. It was teamwork that did it. That's all there is to it!"

She kissed him and replied, "You really are a hero! *Our* hero. Thank you so much." The girls came back with the police, who entered the cabin dragging the other culprit, now wearing handcuffs.

"We caught this one running down the road," said one of the officers. "Your girls identified him as the other half of this twosome. We'll need you to file charges at the station tomorrow when you feel up to it. We know this was a terrible ordeal." The man on the floor began to groan with pain, as the police handcuffed him.

"Excuse me, officer," said Tony. "May I have my knife back? It belongs with a very old set and I would really like it returned if possible."

"Of course, sir. No problem."

"Let me get it, Tony," said Tia. "I'm a nurse, and I'm trained to handle this type of situation. You can observe this new medical procedure. I've just been waiting patiently for the right time to try this out!" She walked over to the man on the floor and kicked the knife as hard as she could. He screamed in pain, begging for mercy. The police officers pretended not to see or hear what was going on. Tia then grabbed the knife with both hands and yanked it from the man's shoulder. Again he screamed, as blood poured from the wound. The officers then dragged the two men off. Tia cleaned the antique knife and handed it back to Tony. "Okay, everyone, the excitement is all over. Let's all try to get some sleep."

Even though they knew sleep would be impossible, the weary group returned to their respective rooms to finish out the night. Lett knocked on Tony's door and went in. She strolled up to where he was sitting and kissed him on the cheek. "I love you,

A Star of Honor

Tony!" she said, running from the room.

"Well, I love you too, baby-san!" he answered, as he closed his eyes to get some rest. Sleep quickly found him as his insides filled with pride.

Chapter 24

Tony was gently awakened by a kiss on the cheek, and the aroma of freshly brewed coffee. "Good-morning, good-looking! Did you sleep in that chair all night?"

"Well, I suppose I'm guilty. First I couldn't sleep, and then I fell asleep . . . all in that order."

"Oh, I see. Anyway, are you hungry?"

"Sure! I'll eat anything but chicken!"

"We have bacon and eggs, or hotcakes. What'll it be, airman?"

"Are you on the menu, mamma-san?"

"Don't tempt me, Tony. After the happenings of last night, a lady could be swayed very easily in that direction."

"Now, Tia, remember our pact, okay? Besides, I'll always respect you as a lady."

"Yes, Tony, the point is well taken . . . would you like a little breakfast now?"

"Yes, ma'am. Now is a pretty good time to have some of that Tia-style cooking!"

A Star of Honor

"Sorry to disappoint you, buddy, but Lisa and Lett have decided to make breakfast for you. You're an important man around these Ramos women, you know!" Tia wheeled his chair into the kitchen area and up to the table. The girls had prepared a breakfast of bacon, eggs, and toast. Tony was impressed.

"Wow, ladies! This is a meal fit for a king. Got any coffee?"

"You know we have coffee, silly man. How could you miss the smell of it in the air?" said Tia.

"Do you like our breakfast, Tony?" asked Lisa.

"Sure do. Everything is just great! So, what kind of plans do you have for the rest of the weekend, mamma-san?"

"I thought we would just relax and enjoy the beauty of this wonderful mountain city. Is that all right?"

"Ain't you girls scared to walk around outside after what happened last night?"

"Not with a big, strong, handsome tough-guy like you around, Tony!" answered Tia. Tony blushed and munched happily at his food, rudely slurping his coffee.

"Yes, sir. Sure is some great chow!"

After breakfast clean up, the group headed to town in the jeep, to rediscover the rest of their vacation. They stopped at the police station to file charges against the intruders. Then they had fun in the busy market place sampling Filipino delicacies. Tony turned up his nose at the thought of eating such delights as fermented bird eggs. Tia took photographs with an old box camera, once belonging to her father. Tony clowned with her by making faces. "Be serious, Tony! This film is costing money to get developed!"

"I don't like pictures, Tia. So don't take any more of me, okay?"

"Just one more, Tony. Smile!" He pretended to be angry, but managed a big smile just prior to the click.

"Are you finished now?"

"Yes . . . are you happy now, killjoy?"

A Star of Honor

"Very."

They continued through the outdoor market place, looking at everything for sale, from livestock to American made black market items. Lisa picked up a yellow, hand-stitched, local made shirt from a table. It was covered with intricate embroidered designs. She handed it to Tia, who wasted no time holding it up against Tony to check the size. "This looks about right."

"Not another shirt!" he balked.

"Just be quiet, okay? We'll make a Filipino out of you yet!" she smiled. They stopped for lunch at a restaurant which overlooked the majestic mountain peaks. Tia ordered a complete Filipino meal with small fried eggrolls called Lumpia, and a cheeseburger for Tony. They each had a glass of beer and the girls drank bottled soft drinks. Tony pointed out over the horizon, as a hawk soared through the clouds and across the endless blue skies.

"Look how free it is, while I'm confined to this wheelchair."

"Don't worry, Tony. I have faith you'll walk again. And so *you* must also have faith . . . understand?"

"Yes, ma'am . . . I guess so. A small boy selling trinkets, approached Tony with his wares. His clothing was torn and dirty. His shiny black hair was cropped close to his scalp. Tia tried to chase him away, but she was stopped by the urgency of Tony's grip. "Bring him here, Tia!" Tia motioned for the boy to come closer. He moved in slowly, remaining cautious. He seemed to look scared and unsure of what the American in a wheelchair would want of him. Tony produced from his wallet, twenty dollars worth of Philippine pisos. He took the whole box of things the boy was selling, and handed him the money. Tia became upset, feeling Tony was wasting his money on a boxload of junk he didn't need. The boy snatched the money and thanked him, running off into the crowd.

"Why did you do that, Tony? That's more money than he's seen in his whole lifetime? It wasn't worth but twenty pisos . . .

A Star of Honor

never twenty dollars, you crazy G.I."

"That kid looked so hungry. I keep seeing little children like that over and over in my dreams. They roamed Vietnam day and night, most of them always starving, and orphans of the war. They had to steal to survive, many died. I remember most, the little girl I found laying in the street after an explosion. She'd lost a leg picking up a booby-trapped soda can, intended for a G.I. like me! Her little hands hugged my neck and with a weak voice, she told me her mother said her daddy was an American. She looked into my eyes and asked if I was her daddy. She knew I must be, because no one else cared about her. I told her in Vietnamese that I was *him*. She died in my arms, Tia! All I could do was cry. People passed by . . . ignoring us. Finally, some church missionaries took her body from me. I cursed God. Why he let those little kids suffer like that . . . I just never understood. I decided at that moment . . . there wasn't any God. My heart goes out to all those kids. They found me . . . even here. So many children . . . so little help."

"Tony, I had no idea," answered Tia softly. "You never told me, but I think you're a very good man to care about others. You see? I learned something from *you*, in my own country!"

"Let's go, Tia. I think I had enough of this, okay?"

"Okay, good-looking. We'll go home now."

Tia paid and they departed the restaurant, loading many items they bought into the jeep. They spent the remainder of the weekend learning about each other. On Sunday, they locked up the old secluded cabin and headed down the mountain road. Although it started off as a nightmare everyone would have liked to forget, they would always reflect on this time together with fondness. The hot sun beat down on the travelers once again. The dusty road to Angeles City and the air base, beckoned to them. They prepared to depart from the beautiful daydreams of Baguio, reluctantly returning to the bitter realities of turbulent times.

Chapter 25

Nightfall approached as they returned home. Tia dropped off her sisters at her mother's house, then brought Tony to the base. It upset him to go back to his hospital bed, but he knew it was something that had to be done. When he was wheeled to the room, he noticed the bed next to him was occupied. Tony made plenty of noise, attempting to wake his new roommate. He then spotted the gold lieutenant's bars affixed to the collar of a uniform hanging on the door. "Tia!" yelled Tony. "They put a fucking officer in my room! What kind of shit is this?"

"Take it easy, Tony. He won't be here for very long."

"Oh, swell! You mean you knew this guy was coming and didn't even tell me about it? What kind of friend are you, anyway?"

"Tony, stop picking on me, okay? I debated on telling you, but I just couldn't bear to spoil the weekend before it even got started."

"Well, who is he anyway?"

"He's an Air Force pilot who flew B-52 missions over North

A Star of Honor

Vietnam. His aircraft was shot down while bombing Hanoi. He was the sole survivor of the crash, and was taken prisoner. He escaped from captivity and made it back to South Vietnam. Go easy Tony . . . he was a POW for three years."

"What's his name, mamma-san?"

"His name is Eric Lane, and as you can see, he's a lieutenant."

"Hell, he looks like a college wimp to me! You sure he broke out of a POW camp?"

"And what kind of wimp are you, good-looking?"

"I ain't no wimp! Whatever possessed you to say such a thing?"

"Just as you're not a wimp, the same should apply to him. Give him a chance, okay?"

"Chance hell! That's what you asked me to do with Spike . . . and he died. Maybe I'm just bad luck on people."

"Oh, stop it! Iron out your differences and go to a neutral corner."

"Oh, real cute!"

"Enough now, Tony! I must go to work, as soon as I change, that is. In the meantime, make the best of this, *understand*?"

"Yes, ma'am. Just keep him on *his* side of the room!"

"Oh, Tony, quit being such a baby. He's no different than you. He's a man, nothing more. He puts his pants on the same way you do . . . one leg at a time! Be good . . . for once," she pleaded, kissing him on the forehead. "See you later!"

"Right, mamma-san, later." Tia left the room to get ready. Tony glared at the officer who was snoring, as though he didn't have a care in the world. He soon awoke, and caught Tony staring.

"Hi! Eric Lane's the name. I just got here today."

"So I see," interrupted Tony, refusing to shake the man's outstretched hand.

"Did I do something wrong, buddy?"

A Star of Honor

"Well, I'll be honest with you, I just never had any use for officers, that's all."

"Right, me too! I was prior enlisted. I used to be a staff sergeant. I finished college on active duty and was accepted into Officers Training School to become a pilot. I don't know how long I'll be here . . . but I hope we can be friends."

"Did you really get shot down?"

"Boy, word really travels fast around here. Yes, I did. My whole crew was killed except for the tail-gunner. He was shot when the VC saw his chute. He always wore a Chicago Cubs baseball cap . . . that's how I knew it was him. I was on the ground already, and watched the tracers tear into him before he hit the trees. I'm sure he didn't make it."

"So, what aircraft did you fly?"

"I flew a 'BUF' as a co-pilot."

"I thought you flew a B-52?"

"I did! BUF is short for Big-Ugly-Fucker. Same-same as a B-52."

"I knew that. I used to be a mechanic. I never worked on *them* though. They always flew over, but none ever stayed long. They just shit on the gooks and left!" he smiled. "You were stationed at Anderson, on Guam, right?"

"Right, Guam. Say, I didn't catch your name."

"That's 'cause I never told it to you. I thought officers were supposed to be smart! My name is Tony." He offered his hand. Eric reached across the gap between the beds and clasped hands.

"Say, Tony! That sure was a cute little thing that brought you in here!"

"I thought you were sleeping! And you can keep your meathooks off her. She's taken!"

"Oh, she's got a boyfriend?"

"Right! Me!" answered an irate Tony.

"She's an officer! She ain't supposed to be messing with enlisted men. She could get into serious trouble."

A Star of Honor

"As you can see, lieutenant, the Air Force can't do much to hurt me . . . any more than this. I got nothing to lose if I rearrange your face. I said she's taken, and I mean it . . . *sir*!"

"Hell, I can see this is going to be a longer stay than at the Hilton!"

"New York Hilton?"

"Nope . . . Hanoi Hilton."

"That's right, Tia did mention you were a POW."

"*Ex*-POW! And who's Tia?"

"Right, ex-POW . . . she's that good-looking captain you agreed not to mess with."

"Okay, Tony, you win . . . you lucky bastard!"

"Oh yeah, Eric, I almost forgot. If you meet up with a Dr. Jacobson, major-type, disregard everything he says to you. The guy's a real armpit!"

"I'm afraid I already met the man, and I agree. I had a different area of the body in mind though!"

"Say, Eric, you like blonds?"

"Sure do, why?"

"I can fix you up with another nurse. Her name's Samantha. She ain't a real prize . . . but she ain't a dog either!"

"How can you perform this great fix-up, Tony?"

"Let's just say, I got a lot of pull with her boss!"

"Don't tell me . . . Tia, right?"

"Right! Besides, Eric, she's more your speed! You couldn't keep up with Tia anyway."

"Why do you say that?"

"Well, lieutenant, the way I see it . . . you have to learn how to crawl, before you can run with the heavyweights, like me!"

"I see what you mean, Tony. I knew that Tia chick was hot for you anyway."

"How so?"

"Well, you already know I wasn't sleeping when you came in. I never had a female captain even give me a second look . . .

A Star of Honor

let alone kiss me. That one sucked off a piece of your forehead, like she might have a deed to the property! My mama didn't raise no fools! Boy, times are changing! Captains kissing airmen . . . what next!"

"Would you believe, Sam and Eric?"

They both laughed and shook hands once again. Tony was reluctant to make friends with an officer, but he agreed with Eric's philosophy. Times were changing in the Air Force, and even hardcore Tony decided to change right along with them. Besides, this Eric guy really didn't seem too bad for an officer. Tony decided to settle down and accept friendship together with change, hoping all things considered, would work out for the best.

Chapter 26

The unmistakable sound of Tia's voice broke the silence that once existed on the ward. "Hi, boys!" she said, as she pushed open the door entering the room. "I see you guys are talking to one another! That's wonderful!"

"I'm hurting, Tia. Shoot me up, mamma-san."

"Okay, Tony, I have it right here." She gave him the injection, then turned around to put a thermometer into Eric's mouth. "You feeling better, lieutenant?"

"When can I get out of here, nurse?"

"I've been told you'll have surgery tomorrow to reset that broken leg you got in the plane crash. Dr. Jacobson said they'll have to break the bones again."

"Will it hurt?"

"I assure you, you won't feel a thing. Don't worry about it."

"I'd ask you to hold my hand, nurse, but Tony said you're his girl."

"Oh, is that what Tony said?"

"You mean it isn't true?"

A Star of Honor

"I've never known Tony to lie. He's also very good with a Filipino throwing knife! I'd listen to him if I were you. He's very tough and just a little bit crazy, so be careful. Lieutenant, we're very close . . . Tony and I. We aren't lovers, but he's assigned himself the job of being my protector."

"How can a guy in a wheelchair protect anyone?"

"Believe me when I tell you, try to keep Tony in a friendly mood. His troubles in the bush were different from yours, but I'm sure that common bond between you will show itself. Just don't anger him, okay?"

"Okay, Tia."

"You *will* address me as captain or nurse. Is that clear, lieutenant?"

"Yes, ma'am. Perfectly clear." She covered both men with clean, white top sheets and promptly left the room to work the ward. Tony was drowsy from his shot, but talked with Eric anyway.

"Don't mess with that girl, Eric! She's dynamite waiting to explode!"

"How come she took you?"

"Well, sir, some of us got it . . . and some of us ain't!"

"Yes . . . and you need to show me just exactly what *it* is, Tony!"

"Eric, what was it like . . . being a POW, I mean?"

"Not good. When our plane went down in the jungle, I hid in the tree cover for the night. The next day, the V.C. were beating the bushes looking for me. I guess they had a knack for smelling Americans or something. When I looked up, I was surrounded by gooks. One of them hit me across the face with a gun-butt. I felt it rip my skin to the bone, and I couldn't walk on my left leg."

"Was it broken?"

"Yeah . . . several places. I passed out, I think from shock."

"You think?"

A Star of Honor

"Well, I can't exactly remember all of what happened. They threw water on me and yanked me back up to my feet. They tied a vine around my neck and pulled me through the shrubs. When I fell, they dragged me. I was beaten and kicked until I got up again. They made me go through the villages we entered with a sign around my neck."

"What kind of sign?"

"I found out later it said I was a CIA murderer of the Vietnamese people. I was forced to walk barefoot over glass and through a gauntlet of old men, women, and children. They hit me with bamboo rods and spit on me."

"Those gook bastards!" yelled Tony. "Did they lock you up after that?"

"No, that was only the first stop. I was marched for days through many villages in the same manner. When we finally reached Hanoi, I was begging them to shoot me. Then came the interrogation process! Officers seemed to get a more thorough working over. I followed the Code of Conduct to the letter. I handed the gook henchman my Geneva Convention card which gave them strict instructions on how to treat American prisoners of war," he said sarcastically.

"Right, I get the picture. Then what happened?"

"He tore up the card and threw it in my face. I told him my name, rank, and serial number. He kicked my broken leg and seemed to enjoy it when I screamed in pain. He punched me until I lost consciousness. They repeated this for days, trying to make me sign some silly bullshit saying I was a criminal."

"Did you sign it?"

"Fuck, no!" he snapped. "I spit on it and they kicked me in the nuts! I was tossed in a cell that resembled an animal cage, with straw mats on the floor. I knew there were other Americans there, but I couldn't see them. Each cell was totally secluded from the others, so we tapped on the walls in a special code to communicate."

A Star of Honor

"Did they ever let you see a doctor?"

"Ha! Are you kidding? That's why I walk this way. The leg healed crooked and the infection, together with the high fever that followed, damn near killed me. The food was some kind of rice slop I think they pissed in. I lost twenty-five pounds in the first month. I would have sold my soul to the devil for a cheeseburger or even a warm can of beer."

"I know that feeling, Eric. The pain, the hunger, the hate. I wasn't a POW, but I've been there. I know exactly what you're saying."

The two men became emotionally close that hot, humid evening. They exchanged stories of their experiences in Vietnam, and wept together over a savage war that left them beaten, but not broken. They found the common bond Tia mentioned, and they knew a brotherhood would follow for as long as they would remember.

Chapter 27

They talked into the early morning hours, only to be interrupted by the rude entrance of Major Jacobson. "Well, Lane," he smirked. "When I get through with you tomorrow, you'll wish you were back in that POW camp."

"Excuse me, sir? What are you trying to say?"

"Too bad you tied in with this Magnacavello bastard. He's been nothing but trouble since he got here." Tony pretended to be asleep, while trying to emulate realistic snoring. Jacobson continued to badger the young lieutenant, with tales of terrible consequences which could result from the surgery he was to endure in a few hours.

"Are you sure you're a doctor?"

"I *could* have you up on charges for a remark like that!" growled Jacobson.

"Forgive me, major . . . I just don't know what came over me. No disrespect was intended."

"Don't let it happen again, lieutenant!" Tony could stand no more of the abuse he was listening to.

A Star of Honor

"Eric! Don't kiss his ass like that! Major, why don't you get the hell out of here . . . while you still can walk!"

"Oh, look who's back in town! Are *you* walking yet, hero?" After checking Tony's chart, he was feeling very brave knowing the airman was recently sedated with morphine. He turned his back on Tony to continue where he left off with Eric. Tony reached down beneath his covers to retrieve his favorite new toys . . . the throwing knives. He carefully removed the largest one from the case.

"Leave him alone, you horse's ass!"

"Lieutenant, I order you to turn your back and forget what you're about to see and hear," said Jacobson. "Mistakes happen on operating tables, so keep in mind what I'm telling you."

"What the hell are you up to, major?"

"Just go to sleep and don't worry about it, lieutenant." He walked over to Tony with a clenched fist, fully intending to hit him. "I'm gonna punch your lights out, hero!" he yelled. Tony's education came from the streets, and he sensed the major's would-be attack. When Jacobson was close enough to him, Tony grabbed the lapel of the doctor's hospital coat, and pulled him onto the bed. With knife in hand, he cut the bottom of his stethoscope completely off. Jacobson screamed for mercy as he saw the anger glaring in Tony's eyes. "Help! Security! Please help me! This airman is crazy!"

"Oh god, not again!" came Tia's voice from the hall, as she ran into the room, a security policeman behind her. Together, they got Tony to partially release the major. "Let go of him!" she screamed. Upon hearing Tia's plea, Tony let the major get up.

"Guard! That airman threatened me with a knife and I want him thrown in jail!" The security guard took the knife and secretly passed it to Tia.

"What knife was that, sir?" he asked.

"Well, I don't know what he did with it now, but that lieutenant will swear I was being attacked."

A Star of Honor

"Is that true?" asked the guard.

"Well, actually . . . I never saw or heard anything. Don't I follow orders good, major?" said Eric, displaying a sly grin.

"You'll pay for this, you fool!"

"What do you have in mind, major . . . torture?" Eric quickly replied. "No biggie, I gave already!" Jacobson readjusted his clothing and went through the motions of dusting himself off.

"Don't forget the surgery, asshole. I always win in the operating room."

"Are you threatening my patient, doctor?" asked Tia.

"Nope, just explaining accidents do happen, that's all."

"Then you remember this, *asshole*," replied Tia calmly. "If this man comes back from his operation with even a head cold he didn't have before . . . I wouldn't suggest you go off base for *any* reason. It could be very hazardous to *your* health."

"Is that a threat, captain?"

"No, sir. Not a threat . . . but a fact of life in the Philippines. Accidents do happen, as you were so nice to remind us, doctor. You keep that in mind, while Lieutenant Lane is on the table." Tia handed the knife back to Tony and smiled. "Great stunt. I owe you a spanking for this!"

"Sorry, mamma-san, I guess I just lost my temper a little." Jacobson headed for the door mumbling under his breath.

"First I get threatened by an airman with a weapon, then it's denied by a blind lieutenant, and now, one of my nurses is leading the Filipino mafia! Holy shit!" Upon his departure, he turned to Tia and remarked, "You'll pay for this, Tia. I'm going to hurt you good!" Before Tia could open her mouth in reply, Tony threw the knife in the major's direction. It stuck into the wall, narrowly missing his left ear. The major paused, looked at the knife protruding from the plaster, and left. He knew he couldn't win and leaving quickly was the best idea he'd had all night.

"Tony, I don't believe you did that! I need to take those away from you. I created a monster, sheesh!"

A Star of Honor

"Thanks, captain. Thanks, Tony," said Eric. "Tony, you really got some brass balls! Oops, sorry, nurse . . . slipped with my language."

"That's okay, Eric. Nothing I haven't heard before, right, Tony?"

"Right, mamma-san."

"Oh, by the way, Eric, you can call me Tia. Welcome to my nut-house . . . I mean ward." Tia reached over to the security policeman and kissed his cheek. Tony noticed the man was a Filipino in the U.S. Air Force. The name tag on his fatigues read: RAMOS.

"Do you know this guy, mamma-san?"

"You might say that. Guys, meet my cousin, Jorge Ramos."

"Well, I'll be damned!" said Tony. "No wonder we ain't in jail." Jorge pulled the knife from the wall and handed it back to Tony.

"Quit tearing up my cousin's ward, okay?"

"You got it, Hoss!" replied Tony. "And thanks." Jorge just nodded as he walked out the door with Tia. She turned briefly and said, "You guys behave now. It's time for me to go home! Please, Tony, no more damage, okay?"

"Okay, baby. Take care." She blew him a kiss as she left, and Tony blew one back. The two roommates settled back to take a nap. Tony clutched his knives close beside him, and drifted off into a state of contentment.

Chapter 28

Eric and Tony were awakened by the noisy orderlies coming to take Eric to surgery, everything being done under the watchful eye of Samantha. "Good-morning, fellas!"

"What the hell's so good about it, Sam?" answered Tony.

"Are you here to take me to the operating room, pretty lady?"

"I don't believe we've met, lieutenant. Yes, I'll be seeing you get to the O.R. on time. By the way, you're very cute."

"Heck, ma'am. Very kind of you to say that."

"It's the truth, lieutenant."

"Would you mind calling me Eric?"

"No problem, Eric. They call me Sam, so I guess you can too!"

"Honored, ma'am. You have the prettiest blue eyes I've ever seen."

"I think you two are going to make me throw up!"

"Shut up, Tony! No one rattled your cage."

"Sam?" asked Eric. "Will you be there when they get done

with me today?"

"Sure, Eric. I'll be the first thing you see when you wake up."

"Now I'm positive I'm gonna puke!"

"Cut it out, man!" pleaded Eric. "Can't we have a little privacy here?"

"Sure, jerk. I'll just get up and walk down to the bar and get a beer!"

"I'm sorry, Tony. I kind of forgot for a minute."

"Don't worry about it, Eric. I guess I should be getting used to this by now."

"Okay, Lieutenant Lane. It's showtime!" She gave him an injection and the orderlies helped move him off the bed and onto a gurnee.

"Say, Tony, did you really toss a knife at Jacobson?"

"You mean you heard already?"

"Heck, Tony, it's all over the hospital! I think you should have cut off his balls!"

"Sam! That's not like you . . . talking that way."

"I guess I've about had it with this place. Even things *you* do, don't surprise me anymore! Okay, guys, wheel him out. I know this is hard, Tony, but please try to stay out of trouble until I get back."

"Don't worry, Sam. I won't wreck anything . . . at least not until I see you again!"

"I'm sure I can count on that. Right, troublemaker?"

"Take care of my roomie. He ain't really a bad dude!"

"You bet, Tony. I'll take good care of this guy," she said, as she squeezed Eric's hand. "Before, during, and after his surgery!" she winked. Tony nodded his approval and winked back as Eric was slowly moved towards the door.

"Hey, Eric!"

"What now, man? Can't you see I'm busy?"

"Can I have your supper? You'll probably be sleeping all evening anyway."

A Star of Honor

"Sure, Tony, what the fuck? Oops, sorry, Sam . . . can't seem to control my nasty mouth these days."

"Don't worry about it, Eric. You have every right in the world to talk the way you want to, considering all you've been through. Besides, how could you help it . . . bunking next to *Mr. Mouth*, over there."

"You're a real lady, Sam. Can I buy you dinner after the show's over?"

"Sounds good to me, buddy! But let's talk about it later, okay?"

"Okay, pretty blue eyes. Let's get this show on the road!" Tony watched as they disappeared down the winding corridor. His thoughts drifted to better times of when he was able to walk. Eric's operation lasted until late afternoon. Tony dropped the *LIFE* magazine he was reading, on the floor by accident. It angered him he couldn't reach down far enough to pick it up. He beat on his legs with both fists in utter disgust. With determination, he pulled himself into a sitting position, and let both legs dangle off the side of the bed. He pushed himself slowly forward, firmly taking hold of the steel bed post. He inched forward a bit more, until his feet reached the green and white tiled floor. Tony tried, using every ounce of strength he could find, to stand up. He felt nothing, either in his legs or his feet. He stood for a few seconds, and tried to move one of his limp legs forward. He lost his balance and fell to the floor like a ton of bricks, pulling over the nightstand and breaking the lamp with a deafening crash. Samantha, now escorting Eric back was distracted by the noise. She ran as fast as she could in Tony's direction. "Tony!" she yelled, kicking open the door. "Where are you?"

"Down here, Sam!"

"Oh my god! What have you gone and done now? Tia will have my butt for this!"

"Sam, quit griping and get me back into bed!" His head was bleeding just above the right eye and bruises were beginning to

A Star of Honor

appear on his arms and legs from the devastating fall.

"Put your arms around my neck. Tony did as he was told and allowed himself to be helped.

"Guess I fucked up good this time!"

"I guess you did," she answered, as she pulled his legs up and slid him under the sheets.

"I'm hurting really bad, Sam."

"Okay, I understand. But first things first, we have to stop that bleeding." She pressed the call button and two orderlies ran in.

"Yes, ma'am?" they responded in unison.

"Get this head wound stopped right now! And keep an eye on this guy so I can get him a shot." The orderlies followed her instructions as Samantha went and then returned with Tony's morphine. She examined the wound. "I don't think stitches will be required. You're a lucky guy. You might have really gotten hurt, pulling a dumb stunt like that! Why did you do it?"

"Sam, I can't take this shit anymore! I refuse to accept never walking again."

"I'm sorry, Tony . . . I'm really sorry. It's in God's hands now. Please don't try this again! I don't think my heart could stand it!" He was sedated, and his top sheet was pulled back over him. Samantha strapped Tony in his bed to keep him from falling out or getting up again, and then went to retrieve Eric, who was still sound asleep in the hallway. The orderlies helped put the pilot back into his own bed, then secured the side rails. "I want one of you to stay in this room until Captain Ramos gets on duty. Is that clear?"

"Yes, ma'am!" snapped the orderly in charge.

"Samantha left the room with the other orderly, all the while thinking about what kind of excuse she would have to offer Tia about this latest incident. She felt she had handled it well, and went back to the ward wondering what troublesome tricks Tony would be up to next.

Chapter 29

Hours passed and Eric started to come out of his anesthesia. Sam was waiting by his bedside as promised. "Hi, cutie!"

"Hi, Sam," he answered with slurred speech. "I feel like I got one kingsize hangover!"

"You will for a while, Eric. Don't try to get up just yet, and don't get that cast wet, okay?"

"Yes, ma'am! Where's Tony?"

"He's right there in his bed, can't you see him?" Eric focused his eyes on Tony and thought he was dreaming.

"Holy cow! Who beat the crap out of you?"

"Take it easy, Eric . . . it's cool. I guess you could say I beat the crap out of myself! I fell out of bed."

"Damn, Tony. You look worse than I feel."

"Right, give the man a little surgery and he comes out a damn comedian."

"Okay, boys, stop fighting!" came a voice from the hallway.

"Oh god! It's Tia. I've been dreading this all day!"

"Hi, good-looking! Hi, Eric . . . Sam."

A Star of Honor

"Hi, mamma-san," said Tony quietly.

"I know you're eager to tell me what happened to you, right?"

"It really was my fault, Tia. Don't blame Sam. I tried to get out of bed to pick up my magazine and I fell. That's all there was to it."

"Were you hurt bad, honey?"

"No, not really . . . just my pride. Looks worse than it actually is."

"And how are you doing, Eric?"

"Fine, ma'am . . . I think."

"Sam?" asked Tia. "Would you mind taking Eric for a little wheelchair ride?"

"I don't mind . . . if he doesn't."

"I don't mind at all, pretty lady. Will you let me buy you some supper?"

"Oh, Eric! That would be simply wonderful!" Tia and Sam helped put Eric into a wheelchair. Samantha happily pushed him to the cafeteria with a starry look in her eyes.

"What's up, mamma-san?"

"You're very perceptive, Tony. You figured out I wanted to talk to you privately. It's about Jim Garver."

"You found him?"

"Well . . . sort of. He was sent to St. Albans Naval Hospital in New York, for rehabilitation."

"Then he did survive?"

"Right, good-looking, he did. I sent a wire to inform him you also survived, and what your present condition is. I told him you received the Silver Star, and he now knows you're in the Philippines. When will you clear up this mystery for me, good-looking?"

"Perhaps never, Tia."

"Tony, that just isn't fair!"

"I just can't talk about it yet, mamma-san. But I will . . . I

A Star of Honor

promise."

"You damn well better, Magnacavello! I got a helluva lot of time invested in you. You owe me at least that much!"

"What about the things that belong to Jim? Do you think I should send them to him?"

"No. Let's just wait and see, okay?"

"Okay, mamma-san. I'll do that."

"*Now*, I want the truth about your accident."

"That *was* the truth."

"Don't bullshit me, airman . . . I won't have it! Now talk! The truth!"

"Okay, Tia, you win . . . as usual. I tried to get up and walk."

"And did you?" she asked in an excited tone of voice.

"I fell flat on my face when I moved my leg!"

"Was there any feeling at all?"

"Well, the flight didn't bother me one bit, baby. The goddamned landing was hell though!"

"No, silly, I mean was there any feeling in your limbs or toes?"

"Nope . . . not that I can remember."

"You aren't ready yet, good-looking. Don't push it, okay? You're a stubborn Italian, and I'm confident you won't give up. It'll come . . . trust me."

"Well, mamma-san, you're the only one I do trust!" Samantha pushed open the door, bringing Eric back to his bed.

"I have to go now," she said. "Time for me to get off duty. I enjoyed supper!"

"My pleasure, ma'am. Let's do it again sometime!"

"That would be *my* pleasure, cutie!" She kissed Eric on the cheek and left the room with Tia to facilitate the change of shifts.

"See 'ya later, guys!"

"Okay, mamma-san. Sure could use a nice back rub," he grinned. Tia shook her head and smiled at Tony.

"What a nut you are! Get some rest, okay?"

A Star of Honor

"Okay, mamma-san, we will."

"Try to stay in bed this time, sport!" she said with a smile, as she walked away giggling.

Tony nestled back into his *LIFE* magazine and finished the rest of Eric's supper tray. His thoughts strayed back to Vietnam and Jim Garver. He wondered if they would ever meet again. He hoped that after his ultimate sacrifice for a friend, that the friend would at least send him a get-well card. Eric went to sleep with thoughts of Samantha fresh in his dreams. Tony was happy in the thought he kept his promise to Jim, and convinced himself despite his suffering, he would have no hesitation about doing it all over again . . . to save the life of another.

Chapter 30

The talk of Jim Garver's whereabouts drove Tony into another nightmare. He tossed and turned in agony, reliving his painful experiences. Tia checked on the two airmen as she came to review their charts. She decided not to wake Tony right away, hoping instead to learn more about him from his dream. She sat next to him on the bed with her arms around his sweating body. He was going through the motions of having a fight with someone, as though acting out a part in a movie. "My poor baby," she said. "I wish I could take away the hurt you suffered . . . and what you're going through now." Then she looked on in amazement, for in the midst of his obvious agony, he moved his toes. It was for a brief moment, but unmistakable. Tony returned from his trance in a cold sweat, tears rolling down his cheeks.

"Where am I?"

"You're still here, good-looking. In the hospital, in the Philippines. Don't you remember?"

"I thought I was *there* . . . again."

"I understand, Tony. No need to talk about it anymore. Re-

A Star of Honor

lax in my arms, okay?"

"Okay, mamma-san, I will for a little while. This was a bad one. For a minute, I didn't think I was coming out of it!"

"Here, lie back for a bit so I can fix your covers." She gently laid his head on the pillow and stepped down to the floor. She pulled up the sheet tucked in at the bottom of the bed, and lightly scraped across the soles of his feet with a wooden tongue depressor. She prayed for a reaction.

"Stop that, mamma-san! I'm trying to rest . . . quit tickling me!"

"Tony! Are you telling me you felt that?"

"By god, *yes*, mamma-san! You did tickle me . . . didn't you?"

"You bet I did! And you felt it! Do you realize what that means?"

"No . . . not really. What does it mean?" She crossed herself and said a silent prayer, clutching the small gold cross worn around her neck.

"It means, you big dummy, the feeling has come back to your legs. I'm no doctor, Tony, so I can't render a scientific explanation, but I think it's a sign from God. Don't give up hope. Keep on fighting! I've always felt you were blessed somehow."

"Oh, Tia, don't get wacky on me now, okay? I still can't move my legs."

"Give it time, honey. I told you it would happen. I prayed every night for you and I believe God is answering. But let's keep it a secret for now, okay?"

"I really don't think it's any cause to rejoice, but you're right. Whatever happens, it should be kept a secret."

"What's all the commotion, you two?" asked Eric.

"Well, nothing exactly. Due to my intense Italian animal magnetism, this nurse just can't keep her hands off me!"

"Sure wish I had that problem with Sam!"

"How are you doing, lieutenant?"

A Star of Honor

"Just fine, ma'am. But my leg kind of hurts a little, that's all."

"I'll get you a shot."

"Don't be too long, mamma-san. Tia hurried off to the medicine cabinet for two syringes of morphine. She smiled, as she pondered the possibility of Tony walking again. After carefully relocking the glass and metal cabinet, she returned to help alleviate the discomfort of her two patients. Upon doing so, she went back to the ward to deal with the rest of the problems.

Tia was a veteran nurse, with a lot of experience in taking care of the many war victims. She took it in stride, and considered it all in a night's work. She knew deep in her heart, when she finished nursing the G.I.s each and every night, she had given them her all. She always left in the morning with a great sense of pride in her accomplishments. Just knowing they needed her, was the only compensation she'd ever wanted from all this . . . or ever really cared about.

"Eric, are you asleep?"

"No, just thinking."

"About what?"

"How damn good it feels to be out of that camp."

"Yeah, buddy, I can imagine. I never flew a B-52. How was it?"

"Well, speaking from a pilot's point of view, I really liked flying it. I guess they may put me back on the line . . . if the shrink thinks I can deal with it."

"Did it ever scare you, taking off with all that explosive power wrapped around your ass?"

"Tony, I was scared on all the missions I ever flew. The ones over North Vietnam were the hairiest. We always wondered if each trip might be our last. My flights were all flown at night. I had a bad feeling about that last one. It was our one-hundredth mission. We were planning on giving all the rough ones away afterwards. But fate didn't see it that way . . . nor did *Charlie*. We flew too close to a surface-to-air missile site intelligence didn't

117

A Star of Honor

warn us about."

"Is that the one that took you out?"

"That was all she wrote! We took a hit in the tail section. The flight control cables gave way and controlling the aircraft became an impossible job. The tail-gunner reported no casualties, but the loose ammunition in the aft compartment was on fire and could blow at any minute. He couldn't get to the fire and asked urgently for instructions. Major Thompson, the aircraft commander, gave the order to bail out. We went out as soon as we could. I never saw the AC pop a chute. I think he rode her down, but I can't be sure. Me and the tail-gunner were the only people who got out that I knew of. The ammo exploded, and the others never had a chance. We still had a payload of bombs, and the destruction that followed was catastrophic. The concussion rocked the jungle, and the rest of the crew must have died instantly upon impact."

"Were there five crewmembers on board?"

"No, six, counting me," replied the lieutenant, sweat beading on his brow. "I can still picture all of their faces . . . they haunt me at night. I really shouldn't have left the aircraft so soon . . . but I was so scared. I just got out."

"Well, you lived! That's the important thing, Eric!"

"Yes, I lived, but the next three years were a big time world of hurt. I believe dying would have been easier. In the camp, I prayed over and over again for death to claim me quickly . . . but it never came. Each day, they would take the captured bomber pilots to sites of demolished villages, schools, or hospitals. I had no idea we'd bombed civilian targets, and I really didn't think high altitude bombing could be that accurate anyway. There were bound to be some civilian casualties."

"Hell, Eric, no way you could have known. Intelligence gave you the targets, right?"

"True . . . but I'm convinced now those bastards knew damn well what the targets were. Just too much death to write it off as

A Star of Honor

stray bombs. I hated myself for a long time for being a part of it."

"What made you escape?"

"Tony, my friend, I had nothing to lose. After all, what could they do . . . kill me?"

"Yep, something like that."

"During a daylight bombing of Hanoi, the impact of a very close 750-pounder blew open the wall of my cell. Two other POWs were killed in the cells around me. I overpowered a guard, who was taking cover, and strangled him with my bare hands."

"Did you try to spring the others?" asked Tony.

"Didn't have time. I might never have gotten another chance. Had to save my own ass, Tony."

"I can deal with that."

"I traveled at night and slept in the trees by day. I met up with some friendlies, South Vietnamese regulars, that is. They took me to a Marine fire base, and the rest is fucking history. What did you do to rate a Silver Star, Tony?"

"I just don't want to talk about it, Eric!"

"That's okay, Tony. I understand . . . really."

"Get those lights out, you two!" shouted Tia.

"Okay, mamma-san, no biggie. We're out of here! Eric?"

"Yeah, Tony, what?"

"You did a great job, man. You got a lot of guts. I hope everything works out for you."

"Thanks, Tony. I really appreciate that."

"Good-night, Eric."

"Good-night, buddy."

As they clasped each other's hands in friendship, they became immersed in darkness as Eric turned out the light.

Chapter 31

As another morning rapidly approached, Tia was making her final check. An orderly wheeled in trays of breakfast for the two, still sleeping airmen. "Rise and shine my babies!" shouted Tia sweetly.

"Well, *shit*, mamma-san. Is it that time already?"

"I'll be taking you somewhere today, Tony. So eat breakfast quickly, okay?"

"Where are we going?"

"Trust me. You'll see when it's time."

"Then I'll just skip breakfast. Let's go now!"

"If I let you do that, you have to promise me you'll eat a good lunch."

"Okay, I promise, mommy. So let's go already!" Tia asked an orderly to bring in a wheelchair. Together they put him in and the nurse pushed the chair casually down the hall. They soon arrived at the rehabilitation section of the hospital, where disabled American veterans from Vietnam, filled the huge gymnasium-like room. Some were being fitted with artificial limbs, to replace

A Star of Honor

losses suffered as casualties. Others were being taught how to use them in everyday applications.

"Why did you bring me here?"

"I said . . . *trust me*!" She wheeled Tony to another area which had a hot whirlpool bath. "I don't care what the doctor said. I'm accelerating your treatments on my own, and don't you dare breathe a word of this, do you understand? It could cost me my job."

"Yes, baby, I understand. What am I supposed to do, swim in there?"

"Not exactly, Tony. All that's required is that you sit in the bath and let the hot, swirling bubbles do their work." She helped him into a pair of blue shorts and checked the water temperature. With the help of a physical therapist, they lifted Tony from the chair and set him down in the middle of the soothing jets of water, which gently massaged his legs. "How does that feel, Tony?"

"Well . . . *hot*!"

"Just *sit* there and stop complaining, good-looking."

"Can you come here, mamma-san? I have a secret to tell you." She came near to the edge of the tank and put her ear close to Tony's mouth. He reached up, grabbed her by the collar of her uniform, and pulled her into the bath with him. She tried to fight it at first, then relented to the will of the strong, but gentle Italian. In she fell, with a scream and a splash.

"Now, what did you accomplish by doing that, smart-ass?" she asked, pretending to be angry.

"Just a typical smart-ass maneuver, that's all, sweet-thing!"

"I ought to give you my cleaning bill too!"

"Tia!"

"*What?*"

"I can move my toes!"

"Oh, Tony, I think you're imagining things."

"No, mamma-san . . . look!" Much to her joy, it was true.

A Star of Honor

He moved his toes without any outside help, and was attempting to move his legs.

"I knew it! I'm sure it'll happen soon!"

"Don't get *too* thrilled, mamma-san. I don't look for any miracles at all."

"Why must you be such a pessimist all the time? Don't you want to walk?"

"Sure I do! What kind of stupid question is that?"

"Oh, Tony, just *shut up*, okay?" He looked at her soaking wet exterior and grinned. "What's so funny?"

"*You're all washed up in this town, sweetheart!*" Tony replied in a borrowed Bogart accent.

"Very funny!" she answered, playfully tossing a wet sponge, hitting him in the face. They looked deeply into each other's eyes, as he pulled her closer and softly touched her lips with his. "Let me go, Tony. I . . . I . . . mmmmm."

Ignoring her protests, he pressed his body tightly to hers and continued on with his long, slow, sensuous kiss. In the early days of their relationship, she felt a situation like this was wrong. But now, her patient held her very soul in captivity. Her deep desire from within burned feverishly and time as she knew it, seemed to vanish. Tia grew light-headed, practically fainting in his arms. Her heart pulsed to a rapid crescendo, and she felt as though she had been transformed into a beautiful fairy princess, floating freely through the mist of a brilliantly colored rainbow. Although she nearly succumbed to his seemingly satanic charm, the fantasy soon gave way to reality, as she broke free from his embrace and gently pushed him back. "Tony, not now . . . not here, like this. People are watching us."

"Well . . . *when?*"

"When the time is right, good-looking."

"When will that *be*, Tia?"

"We'll both know when, so don't worry about it now, okay?"

A Star of Honor

"Well, you have to admit, baby, we sure got off to a great start, huh?"

"Yes, we did, Tony. Now, let's get you out of this tank before Dr. Asshole finds out."

"Good thinking, mamma-san!" Tia and an orderly helped Tony out of the water, then she wheeled him towards his room. When they passed through the corridor, Jacobson spotted them as he was leaving the doctors' lounge.

"Your uniform is a disgrace, captain!" he yelled. "And what are you doing, sneaking around the ward all wet with this crippled white boy?"

"Are you implying something, major?"

"I heard you and this airman have something going with each other. I think you might have been trying to screw him in the shower or something!"

"That's slander, major! I hope you are prepared to prove that!"

"Sure I can! I also have records showing you sneaked him out of the hospital for some wild orgy up in the mountains! I told you I would make you pay for the way you and this troublemaker have been messing with me."

"Jacobson! You have nothing on her, you stupid asshole!"

"Look, cripple! Why don't you just turn that little brown pussy over to a real man . . . like me! You're only half a man! You couldn't do it any good if you tried!" At that moment, another veteran was being pushed in a wheelchair past Tony, holding a crutch across his lap. Tony reached over, grabbing the crutch.

"Excuse me, brother, but I need to borrow this for a few minutes."

"Sure thing, buddy."

"Thanks, I'll return it in pretty good shape . . . I hope!" Before Tia's and Jacobson's amazed eyes, Tony used all his strength to rise to his feet from the wheelchair. Carefully placing each foot on the floor, and holding onto the borrowed crutch, he stood

A Star of Honor

scowling at the doctor. "This is for Spike! I hold you personally responsible for his death. And for Captain Ramos, who you've continuously offended with your crude remarks! Goddamnit! This is for *everyone* you've ever hurt, you stinking bastard! And last of all . . . it's for *me*. The man you thought you would let die on the operating table. I heard all of it, that night *you* pronounced me dead. I remember how they covered me with a sheet, on *your* orders. It was instant hate for you then, and my will to survive compells me to do what I'm about to do now."

"Let's be reasonable, Tony," pleaded Jacobson.

"Oh, so now I graduated from the *crippled white boy*, to Tony, huh?"

The doctor attempted to run and in so doing, pushed Tia down to the floor. This angered Tony, who quickly swung the crutch in the doctor's direction. "Taste some Italian justice, you son-of-a-bitch!" The crutch crashed into Jacobson's face, knocking his head into the wall. He fell to the floor unconscious and everyone on the ward who surrounded Tony, loudly cheered their approval of the airman's actions. Tony stood, unassisted for the first time in months, holding the crutch over his head, waving it much to the delight of the highly excited mass of patients and hospital staff. He resembled David, standing victorious over a slain Goliath. His body then rocked from side to side, and he fell to the floor, not being able to move. Tia had him carried to his room, and the doctor taken to the E.R.

"That asshole Jacobson will probably figure out a way to get a Purple Heart out of this and be a hero," she pondered. As Tony was placed back in his bed, Tia stroked his head. "Sleep now, my hero. You rest . . . and we'll sort it all out later." She covered him, kissed his forehead, and left.

Chapter 32

Samantha's rounds brought her to Tony and Eric's room. Tony was still sound asleep, exhausted from his ordeal with Jacobson. Eric coaxed his favorite nurse to spend some time with him. "Good-afternoon, pretty lady. I'll volunteer my hand . . . if you'll take my pulse."

"I'm sure you will, lieutenant!" she answered, peering over her glasses in a very studious fashion.

"I missed you, Sam. Where have you been?"

"Well, I've been following the exploits of your famous roommate."

"What kind of trouble did he get into this time?"

"I can't believe you slept through it all, Eric! Tony beat the tar out of Jacobson with a crutch!"

"No! He didn't!"

"He was *magnificent*! You should have seen him . . . the way he stood there and let him have it!"

"Sam, did you say Tony stood?"

"Yep! He got up from the chair and knocked Jacobson right

A Star of Honor

on his butt! It took eleven stitches to close the wound. He also lost a tooth and has a mild concussion."

"Tony did?"

"No, silly. The major did!"

"The major did, what?"

"Oh stop it, Eric. You're just making fun of me now."

"I'm sorry, Sam. Will Tony get in any trouble?"

"Well, ordinarily he would have, but everyone is swearing Jacobson provoked it. Also, Tony was on morphine, and not really responsible for his actions."

"But he actually stood . . . by himself?"

"He was great!" she raved on. "We're all so proud of him."

"Gosh, Sam. Guess I don't have a chance . . . with Tony around."

"A chance for what?"

"A chance to be your boyfriend," he answered, in a shy voice.

"Why, Eric, this is so sudden. And besides, Tony doesn't enter into the picture like that anyway. I like you very much, lieutenant . . . but however, something like this right now would interfere with our careers."

"Oh boy, story of my life."

"What do you mean?"

"Rejection, that's what I mean. Every time I meet a nice lady . . . like you, I think I could spend the rest of my life with, I get turned down."

"If a girl didn't know any better, lieutenant, she might mistake that for a proposal."

"Well, it was, damnit!"

"Why did you pick me? I'm not very pretty, and I spend all of my time reading books."

"Because, lady, I'm in love with you . . . and I just can't help myself. There . . . now I've turned into a complete fool, I guess you can go and have a laugh at my expense."

"Eric, honey, I would never do that. And the truth of the matter is, I think I'm in love with you too."
"Really?"
"Uh huh."
"Then you'll marry me?"
"Well, let's look at it this way . . . if you're crazy enough to want to marry somebody like me . . . then I'm just crazy enough to accept."
"Well, that is just *fucking* great!" came a voice from the next bed. "I suppose I'll have to call a priest to come and marry you . . . just so I can get some goddamn sleep!"
"Tony, you're awake!"
"No shit, Sam. You're still on the ball, I see!"
"Don't talk to my pretty bride like that, buddy!" snapped Eric.
"Settle down, baby. Tony's always like that. Why, that's his way of saying he's happy for us. Isn't it, Tony?"
"Oh fuck, you two! Congratulations! *Now* can a guy get some rest around here?" He shook the pilot's hand and hugged Samantha.
"What's going on here, people?" asked Tia, strolling in unannounced.
"Ain't you gone home yet, mamma-san?"
"No, hot-shot! Your antics caused an awful lot of paperwork for me, and I finally finished it."
"But was it worth it?"
"Yep, good-looking . . . it made my day!"
"Oh, by the way, Tia. These two numb-headed people have decided to get hitched!"
"*What*?! You mean *married*?"
"Did I stutter, Tia? *Yes*! They're getting married!"
"Oh my god! That's so wonderful!" Tia hugged Samantha and Eric at the same time, kissing both of them alternately. "The nurses will give you a shower, Sam."

A Star of Honor

"That ought to be great, Sam! I've had one of her showers before."

"Oh, Tony, stop it! Not *that* kind of shower."

"And what kind of shower was *that*, captain?" grinned Sam.

"Never mind, Sam. Don't listen to him. Must be the drugs he's on. Anyhow, congratulations." The two women hastily left the room to spread the word of the soon-to-be-wedding.

"You think I screwed up, Tony . . . don't you?"

"No, I don't, Eric. Go for the gold, man! I knew you would find a chick . . . one of these days."

"I guess that's a compliment, right?"

"Look, I'll dance at your fucking wedding! Now, can I *please* get some rest?"

"Sure, Tony. I'm just so darned excited."

"Me too, lieutenant. Now let me rest, okay?"

"Okay."

Tony closed his eyes once again, and Eric donned his robe to walk out on the ward, telling everyone he came in contact with about Samantha . . . the wonderful blue-eyed nurse, who had agreed to become the future Mrs. Eric Lane.

Chapter 33

Several days passed, and the hospital was buzzing with the news of the pending marriage. Tony and some of the other men on the ward decided to give Eric a bachelor party. Although parties in the hospital were strictly forbidden, except for major holidays like Christmas, Tony still managed to arrange the festivities, complete with beer. Tia's cousin, Jorge, brought in a quarter-keg of American made brew and potato chips. A bar was discreetly set up under an oxygen tent out on the ward. Even a small stereo-record player mysteriously appeared. The nurses donated sandwiches and Tia looked the other way as they just simply had a good time. Samantha was given a bridal shower by Tia and the other nurses. Each presented her with gifts and personal items they purchased in the base exchange. "We tried to find better things for you, Sam, but the new stock just never seems to come in over here. The war is very hard on all of us, I guess, but we each have to do our part. Here . . . I bought this for you in Manila. I believe a lady should start off her married life looking as sexy as she possibly can for her new husband." She handed Samantha a

A Star of Honor

box wrapped in silver paper. It had a blue bow on top with a card attached. Samantha hastily opened the wrappings and began crying upon seeing the contents. She removed a black silk nightgown, and held it against her body.

"Thank you so much, Tia," she said, still sobbing. "It's so beautiful! But, I think it would look much better on you!"

"That was sweet of you to say, Sam, but up until now, I've always been a bridesmaid . . . never a bride! And I know you'll look just beautiful in it, so enjoy!"

"Tony seems to be stuck on *you*."

"Well, never mind about Tony . . . or me, okay? Let's just have a great time in *your* honor. When is the big day?"

"Well, Eric got his orders already. He's going to be a C-141 transport pilot at Dover, Delaware. He asked for that duty so he can come back here often, to visit me on supply runs. I'll join him in six months when my tour is up. He'll be leaving as soon as his leg heals. I got my reassignment approved already."

"Yes, but when's the big day?"

"Next Friday! We'll be married in the chapel on base and honeymoon in Manila."

"Why not Baguio?"

"No, Tia. We decided on Manila. For some reason, Eric wants to go there. I don't care where it is really. I just can't believe this is happening to me!"

"Even with suffering and sickness all around us, we always seem to maintain our sanity by doing these nice little things for each other. Tony's always telling me what a tough bunch of gals we nurses are. Sometimes I wonder how we keep going like we do." Tia opened a mahogany cabinet and pulled out a complete set of drinking glasses and two bottles of scotch. She set up a small bar on a metal hospital table, as Samantha poured ice into a bucket.

"It was so nice of you to have this for me in the nurses' lounge."

A Star of Honor

"Let's get *blasted*, ladies!" suggested Tia. "We deserve it!" The other women, totalling eight, all joined Tia in a toast to Samantha and Eric. After a few rounds were had by all, they raised their glasses and had yet another toast.

"I propose this toast to *us*! The nurses all over this base, and especially our sisters in Nam," said Jane, the redhead of the group.

"Here! Here!" came the reply in unison. They all raised their glasses once again, then began to reminisce about their experiences with those they treated on their various tours of duty. They laughed and cried at some of the crazy things Tony had done since his arrival. Eyes teared as they all remembered Spike.

"I had to learn the hard way with him," said Tia. "I think lack of morale and a stupid doctor, killed him. I don't care what it takes now . . . a little party, a trip to the mountains, even just a trip outside on the grounds. I think it's *all* important to help the patients recover, both mentally and physically. Just look at Tony! I know he'll be walking on his own soon." She took a sip and pondered that thought. She secretly wept inside, wondering if Tony would be moving on soon like Eric, now that he was recovering. She tried to put it out of her mind and continued to join in the celebration. "Let's drink up girls! Bring your drinks and let's go crash the bachelor party."

"You really think we should?" asked Sam. "It's not very ladylike."

"Hell, yes!" came a unanimous reply.

"Is this a panty raid?" she asked the group.

"Heck, Sam," said Jane. "The only panties that gang of brutes has . . . are what they stole from us! No . . . we want boxer shorts!"

"Let's go, ladies!" yelled Tia. They picked up their drinks and remaining scotch, heading defiantly towards the private *men only* party. They resembled a small lynch mob going to a hanging, and Tia led the raid. They gathered quietly outside the

A Star of Honor

swinging doors so they could peek in on the now, very drunk party-goers. Somehow, Jorge managed to hire a stripper from a local bar to perform, and the party was getting loud and out of control. The nurses weren't one bit happy about the young lady removing her clothing in front of *their* cheering patients. "Morale is one thing, ladies!" screamed Tia. "But *this* is something else!"

"What'll we do about it?" asked Sam.

"I have an idea!" said Tia. "Two of you follow me." Two nurses followed Tia down the corridor where the fire hose was stored on the wall. They unrolled it and dragged it to the swinging doors. Jorge was guarding the doorway against female intruders.

"You can't come in here! Men *only!*" he ordered. Tia gave the signal and Jorge was the first to go, as the water hit him squarely in the chest. The stripper was next to fall, screaming and cursing as she scrambled for her clothes. Tony hit Tia in the face with a sandwich and she retaliated with a signal to the hose-bearers.

"Look out, Tony!" yelled Eric. "*Incoming! Incoming!*" Tony was hit with a torrent of water, sending his wheelchair crashing into the wall. The force of the water soon diminished to a mere trickle, as the outside tank quickly emptied. Taking full advantage of the situation, Tony gave his rowdy group the attack signal. They bombarded the nurses with sandwiches, beer, and any kind of food they could throw. When the frustrations on both sides settled down, they all just laughed until tears poured from their eyes.

"What a mess!" said Tia, still laughing.

"I guess a big G.I. party is in order, huh, mamma-san?" grinned Tony.

"Yes!" she agreed, wiping the sandwich from her face. "But first we need to help you guys finish up that keg! Get rid of the evidence . . . so to speak."

"Well, that's fine by us, right guys?"

A Star of Honor

"Right!" they answered.

All the culprits involved settled down together in the mess they created, to finish up the beer. Tia wondered how she would explain all this to the hospital commander, but decided whatever the consequences . . . it was well worth the trouble. She finally saw her war-beaten patients, and her overworked nurses, having fun for the first time in a long time, and *that* was good enough for her.

Chapter 34

Nurses and patients alike, all pitched in to clean up the remains of the wild parties. Most of the men on the ward, who were not too badly incapacitated by their wounds, were given a pass to attend the wedding. It was scheduled for the following Friday, and everyone promised to be there, both sober *and* on time. Tony was asked to be the best man, and Tia, the maid of honor. Finally, the big day arrived. The chapel was decorated in simple fashion, with white bows, paper bells, and two large brass candlesticks, proudly displaying their flickering candles. The wedding was kept in the strictest military tradition, as requested by the two young lieutenants. When the vows were finalized, a very happy Eric kissed his lovely bride, Samantha.

Upon leaving the chapel, the pair walked beneath two unwavering rows of uplifted crossed sabres, provided by the base honor guard. Rice was thrown as the couple climbed into the familiar red jeep, on loan from the Ramos family. "Good luck, Sam!" said Tia, while giving her a hug and a kiss. "Remember . . . *sexy!*"

A Star of Honor

"Say, Eric!" yelled Tony.

"What is it now, buddy?" came an annoyed response.

"Don't do anything I wouldn't do, bozo! But if you *do* . . . don't forget to name it after me!"

"Hell, Tony! If it's all the same to you . . . I'll just name it after me. You'll just have to make your own, I guess."

"Right, lieutenant. I understand. Good luck to you! Take care of the little lady, I love her like a sister."

"He *fights* with her like a sister, he really means," smiled Tia.

Off they chugged, as a billow of smoke once more poured from the rusted tailpipe, and the noise of a loud backfire prevailed. Tin cans and several pairs of old Vietnam jungle boots, dragged from the rear bumper as the well-wishers waved to the departing couple. When all calmed down, Tia pushed Tony's chair to a quiet place, in the shade of an oak tree which grew behind the chapel. "This is such a nice peaceful place."

"Yes, it is peaceful. What's on your mind, mamma-san?"

"Who said anything was on my mind, good-looking?"

"You never want to get me alone in a quiet place, unless you have something to tell me *or* a big lecture is coming."

"No lecture. I just have lots of things to think about right now, that's all."

"Well, baby, why not just start at the beginning? Now talk to me!"

"I know you can walk now, Tony, so why don't you give up the security you're trying to find in that wheelchair?"

"How do you know whether I can walk or not? You only saw me stand once, and that was to teach a major a lesson. I probably couldn't do it again if I tried!"

"Tony, you never lied to me before! Why are you starting now?"

"Okay, mamma-san, what the hell is bugging you? Now you're calling me a liar. Why?"

A Star of Honor

"Because the orderlies told me they watched you practicing to walk every day since you decked Jacobson."

"I wanted to surprise you, Tia! What the *fuck* is so wrong with that? I thought you would be happy for me!"

"I *am* happy for you, Tony, but . . ."

"But *what*, mamma-san?"

"I feel so ashamed of myself for thinking these thoughts, good-looking, so let's not worry about it, okay?"

"Don't pull *my* shit on *me*! What thoughts are bothering you so bad? Tell me!"

"Well, I'm happy you can walk now, honey. I do appreciate the fact you wanted to surprise me with it, but . . . a very hard-to-deal-with thought *has* been troubling me. It struck me when I talked to Samantha the other day, as she was telling me Eric would be shipping out whenever his leg fully heals. The thought occurred to me that soon, *you* would be leaving . . . when you were able to walk. I suppose I'm more in love with you than I wanted you to know about. I guess now . . . the cat's out of the bag. I'm sorry, that's very selfish and unprofessional of me."

Tony reached over and pulled Tia close to him. He tried to dry her now falling tears with his handkerchief. "I knew *that*, mamma-san. I figured this day would be coming soon, so I tried to prolong it by staying in the chair as long as I could. Please stop crying, baby. I know this is all going to work out . . . somehow."

"Look at us, Tony! We're acting just like two little children. I was feeling so sorry for myself, that I almost forgot to tell you about the wonderful news I have for you!"

"News? What news, Tia?"

"I received a reply to my overseas cable . . . from Helen Garver."

"You mean . . . Jim's wife?"

"Right! They're going to have a baby, and Jim has almost fully recovered from his wounds now. Helen said he insisted on seeing you, and they're coming to the Philippines to do just *that*, in two weeks!"

"Mamma-san, that's just fucking fantastic as hell! I knew he wouldn't forget me, I just knew it! Now, get me out of here, baby! We have lots of planning to do."

"You walking or riding?"

"Riding," he grinned. "Home, James!" he chuckled, as he pointed towards the hospital.

"Okay, Tony. One last time."

"Oh, Tia-san?"

"What now, Tony?"

"Want to get drunk with me?"

"Not a bad proposition, buster! I have some San Miguel in the refrigerator."

"Shit-hot! It's a date! Let's do it!"

"Yes . . . let's."

The couple moved leisurely back to the hospital. Tia pushed his chair as she had done, so many times before. Tony just sat there, enjoying every minute of it, as well as the soft northerly breeze that gently caressed them.

Chapter 35

After returning Tony to the ward, Tia went to retrieve a six-pack of cold San Miguel. This time when she came to his room, she found him sitting on a soft cushioned chair beside his bed. "I got the beer, good-looking. I see you're getting around better now. Are you comfortable?"

"Well, I'm very stiff and I can't really move on my own too well yet."

"It'll be just fine, Tony. With the therapy we have you scheduled for, along with the whirlpool baths, you'll be walking on your own in no time!"

"What about these nasty scars I have all over my back?"

"You're scheduled for your first skin graft in a few weeks. Just try to be patient, honey . . . okay?"

"I'm really trying hard, Tia. It's just I've lost so much of my life between Vietnam and here, I really don't know where to start again. All I do know is . . . I have a helluva lot of catching up to do."

"Tony, don't worry so much about the life you lost over

A Star of Honor

there, just look at the life you've gained! I gather from what you've said about your past, your life really wasn't anything to brag about to start with."

"Well, I was satisfied with it! Say, mamma-san, how about giving up some of the beer, huh?"

"Sure, good-looking. Sorry about that." She opened several bottles, and Tony poured them into two glasses. He handed one to Tia, as he slowly sipped off the foam on his.

"Mmmm, this is some good shit!"

"Yeah, I agree. Not a bad batch, I suppose. Tony, what made you join the Air Force, anyway?"

"Not a very romantic story, I'm afraid. Are you really interested in that crap?"

"Yes."

"Well . . . it's really a long story, 'ya know."

"I have *all* night. Now stop the bullshit and tell me already."

"Okay, mamma-san. Don't get your bloomers in an uproar. I'll tell you!" He settled back into his chair, propping both feet on the small magazine table in front of him. Tia poured them both more beer, while reclining in the chair next to him, putting her feet up as well. "I really had the hots for three things when I was growing up—booze, broads, and exceptionally fast cars! I belonged to a street gang in the city, and we always did wild and crazy things we considered to be cool!"

"Such as?"

"Such as stealing cars! I was very good at it too. I could break into one and hot-wire the ignition . . . in less than a minute!"

"I guess that's record breaking time, Tony, but I really don't care about the statistics. Just tell me what happened."

"Right, baby. One night, I was drinking with a bunch of guys and really felt the urge for speed . . ."

"You mean drugs?"

"No, Tia! Speed as in *cars*! Now quit interrupting me."

"Okay, sorry. Touchy, touchy, touchy. Please go on,

A Star of Honor

Tony."

"I found a really sweet looking Corvette Stingray, just sitting there doing nothing. I lifted it, just as easy as you please."

"You picked it up?"

"I *stole* it, Tia! Quit fucking with me now. I know, that you know, exactly what I'm talking about."

"Okay, then what happened?"

"I drove around drinking beer half the night, cruising the neighborhood looking for chicks. I really thought I was cool too. I got into quite a few drag races that night. The Vette was unstoppable! It blew the doors off everything it raced against. Then I picked up this cute blonde in a mini-skirt."

"Was she pretty?"

"I already said she was cute, okay? She sure had a great set of . . . never mind. Anyway, where was I?"

"You were blowing people's doors off and picking up a blonde . . . I think."

"Right, I was showing off for the chick and went through a red light at the intersection on Grand Central Parkway. Another car clipped me, and we hit two parked cars, flipping over onto somebody's lawn."

"Were either of you hurt?"

"No, we weren't hurt, but she got really scared. I was pinned inside the wreck, and that chick took off running when the cops got there. They got me out of the car and took me straight to jail!"

"Without a trial?"

"Well, a trial would have come later, baby, but they threw me in the holding cell for the night. I used my one phone call to notify my mother. She was so pissed off . . . she hung up."

"Good for her!"

"Say, whose side are you on, anyway?"

"Why, *yours* of course, silly! Then what?"

"My uncle came to the police station to get me out on bail

A Star of Honor

the next day. I think he slipped the judge a bribe or something, 'cause I really thought I was going up the river to prison. When I stood in front of the judge, he asked for my driver's license. I gave it to him and he tore it up on the spot! Then he looked at my uncle while lecturing me, stating he would give me two choices: either I go to prison for five years, or join any branch of service I wanted to."

"So that's when you joined the Air Force?"

"Well, actually I signed up in all the services. The Air Force just got me out of town sooner! So you see, I really wasn't enlisting to be patriotic or anything like that."

"I understand," said Tia, as she poured two more beers. "That's more excitement in one night than I've experienced all my life!"

"That's not funny, mamma-san!"

"Sorry."

"I never did find out what happened to the chick. I guess she got away clean."

"You were a troublemaker even then! That kind of explains the little boy in you now . . . that doesn't seem to want to grow up."

"Real cute, mamma-san. That's easy for *you* to say. I suppose hosing down a hospital ward full of sick people while being drunker than shit was a real grown-up thing to do, right?"

"Not grown-up, Tony, but *very* effective! Besides, that prostitute needed to be cooled down anyway."

"Why does everyone think a stripper is a prostitute?"

"Tony, stop it! It's six of one, and half a dozen of the other. Now, can we please change the subject?"

"Yes, ma'am! Did we drink that whole six-pack already?"

"My god, it looks like we did! Good thing we aren't on duty."

"What's the plan, baby? You think you can make it off base to get home?"

A Star of Honor

"I think so, Tony. I'm a big girl now."

"Well, mamma-san, I have no doubt in my military mind about that, but however . . . I still worry a little about my favorite nurse."

"Don't worry, Tony. I'll just call my cousin, Jorge to escort me."

"Fuck, baby, is he still talking to you after you blasted him with that firehouse?"

"Very funny, Mr. Smart-ass!" Tia got up from the chair to find a phone to call Jorge. She fell to the floor laughing.

"Oh hell! Look who's shit-faced! Just stay down there while I make the call." Tony called to have Tia picked up and taken home. Although Jorge hadn't fully forgiven her, she was still family, and he reluctantly came anyway.

"Let's go, cousin. Your mother is really going to be upset."

"Why do you say that, Jorge?"

"Well, my aunt is not exactly what you would call a *liberated* woman. Everyone in my family is very old fashioned. Drunk women are frowned upon."

"Well, Jorge, I guess we better sober her up then!" They both looked at each other and laughed.

"Hell, Tony! Are you thinking what I'm thinking?"

"You bet! Now comes the paybacks!" Tony got up with the assistance of crutches and helped Jorge carry Tia to the shower room. They set her down on the shower floor and turned on the ice cold water.

"You two will pay for this!" she screamed.

The two G.I.s laughed, knowing full well they had avenged Tia's firehose gag. They also knew, as Jorge escorted a very wet nurse home, that the paybacks would come again. It was moments like this, they all cherished.

Chapter 36

Several weeks seemed to disappear quickly, and Tony's legs became stronger with each passing day. Tia spent long hours with him, sharing both the frustrations and joys, associated with his learning to walk again. Therapy was both exhausting and painful, as Tony fought with every ounce of strength for the few steps he was able to take. Each time he fell, Tia made him get back up and try again. He leaned on her shoulder and inched forward, refusing to give up. "How am I doing, mamma-san?"

"Looks great to me, honey! A little more practice and you'll have it down pretty good!"

"Can we go back to the room now, Tia? I'm getting very tired and I'm really hurting."

"Sure, good-looking. You've worked hard enough for one day. Do you need a shot?"

"I think so, baby."

"Okay then, let's get you onto those crutches."

"Crutches? *What*, no wheelchair?"

"I told you a long time ago, Tony, the free ride is over! You'll

A Star of Honor

have to learn to get around on your own. You need to find independence again. After all, even mother hens have to let their chicks leave the nest sometime."

"Well, ain't that a bitch," complained Tony, grabbing the crutches from her. "Okay, I'm ready . . . let's go." Slowly, they proceeded down the hallway, through the ward and back to his room. Tony was cheered on with words of encouragement by each of the veterans and staff that knew him, as they passed the many rows of neatly made beds. "Tia, isn't this the week Jim and Helen are supposed to come?"

"Tony, I told you a million times, *yes*! Thursday is when they'll arrive. That's the day after tomorrow. So please, be patient, okay?"

"Are you sure it's *this* Thursday?"

"Of course I'm sure, and so should *you* be! You've looked at that telegram they sent twenty times a day since it arrived."

"Well, I don't know about *twenty* times," he answered. "Nineteen might be a closer guess."

"Okay, smart-ass, I get the picture. Well, good-looking . . . here we are!" she said, stopping at his room. "Home, safe and sound."

"Right, home it is." Tia took the crutches and helped him sit down. She relieved his pain once again with morphine and a kiss on the forehead. Tony lay back on the bed staring at the watch belonging to Jim, and the photograph which he guarded with his life. He eagerly anticipated their arrival hoping the reunion would help to ease the agony of the nightmares which terrorized him each and every night. Tony took Tia's advise and waited patiently for his big day.

"Good morning, fella! Rise and shine! It's Thursday! The day you've been waiting for has finally arrived."

"Good-morning, Tia. Are they here yet?"

"Not yet, good-looking, but the C-141 will be landing at 1300."

A Star of Honor

"Tia?"

"Yes, baby?"

"I'm scared."

"What's to be scared of? You waited so long for this to happen. What's wrong?"

"I don't want them to see me like this . . . a cripple, I mean."

"Tony, that's bullshit and *you* know it! Stop the feeling-sorry-for-yourself act. It just doesn't work anymore. So knock it off, airman, and that's an order! Is that *clear*?"

"Yes, ma'am. Clear as mud!"

Tia kissed him, then winked to let him know she understood what he was going through. She stayed close by, keeping his mind occupied until the Garver's arrival. She left the room at 12:45, to greet them. She recognized Jim immediately from the photo she had seen so many times. He was a tall man, at least six feet in height. He walked slowly with his wife's assistance, obviously still in some pain from his healing wounds. His hair was dark brown and his eyes a deep blue. He was wearing his Air Force uniform, adorned with many ribbons, displaying proudly his Purple Heart, which stood out above the rest. Helen wore a blue cotton dress, with a white belt and matching shoes. Her black, plastic-framed glasses made her green eyes clearly visible.

"Are you Captain Ramos?"

"Yes, I am. Welcome to the Philippines!" Jim offered his hand slowly. Tia shook it briskly.

"This is my wife, Helen."

"I'm so very pleased to finally meet you both. Tony has told me so much about you, Jim."

"All *good* things, I hope!"

"Of course, Jim, only good things! Come, follow me. Tony is waiting in his room." They walked to the doorway, and the two men stared at each other in disbelief.

"Jim?"

A Star of Honor

"Tony!" Jim cried out, lunging towards Tony's bed. The two men embraced, as tears streaked their faces. Tia motioned to Helen, and the two women left the two, happy buddies alone. They found each other once again.

Chapter 37

Tony and Jim reminisced about the experiences they shared. With Jim there, Tony seemed to gain a new perspective in dealing with some of his problems. "For a long time I thought you were dead," said Tony.

"For a long time, I thought I was dead too," answered Jim. "If it wasn't for you . . . I would have been for sure."

"I wonder where the girls went?" replied Tony. "I asked Tia to bring us back something to drink."

"You mean the nurse that met us?"

"Yep, that's Tia all right! Ain't she beautiful?"

"She sure is, Tony. Is she yours?"

"Just very close friends, nothing serious. You know what I mean, right?"

"She's a real *piece*, buddy! Forgive me, but I know you better than that. I think there's more to it than meets the eye. I won't harp on it though. You'll tell me when you're ready, I'm sure."

"Helen seems to be a really nice person, Jim. I guess it takes a real *special* lady to be *that* much in love with a mug like you."

A Star of Honor

Both men laughed at Tony's comment. Their friendship ran deep, and each overlooked the other's remarks. Back in Nam, any kind of talk about another man's woman would have been enough to start a brawl . . . and most often did. Tia and Helen soon came back with several six-packs of beer and some of Tia's infamous barbecued chicken. "We're back, good-looking. Did you miss us?"

"Yes, we did! Now where the hell is the beer, woman?"

"Don't mind Tony," she answered, her face turning slightly red. "He likes to show off in front of people."

"Don't apologize for *him*. I've got one just like it, who does the same thing in front of everybody at home! But I love him anyway . . . and I wouldn't trade him for anything in the world!"

"I understand what you're saying, Helen, and you're right! They are really kind of nice underneath those rough-looking exteriors. Guess what I brought you to eat, Tony?"

"If you say chicken, I'm going to *scream*!"

"And what's so bad about my chicken?"

"Nothing, baby. Can we have some beer now?" Tia wasn't sure if Helen would like the San Miguel, so she bought some American brewed beer at the officers' club instead. The two vets didn't care, as long as it was wet and alcoholic, it suited them just fine. Tony relaxed on the bed with a can and the others made themselves comfortable on the soft cushioned chairs Tia dragged in from the nurses' lounge. All was quiet for a while, as the members of the group were each lost in private thoughts. "Well, let's don't all talk at once," joked Tony. Everyone laughed at his remark and the long silence was broken. Helen looked at Tony with tears rolling down her cheeks. She arose, walked over to his bed, and hugged him. She whispered something into his ear and kissed his face. Then she spoke so all could hear.

"I can never thank you enough for what you did, Tony. If you hadn't . . . I would never have been carrying this baby. I would be a widow . . . instead of being a happy wife. Jim and I

A Star of Honor

decided if the baby is a boy, we want to name him in honor of you . . . if you don't object of course."

"That is really very nice of you both. It's an honor I don't really deserve."

"*Quiet*, garlic breath!" said Jim in a loud voice. "Our minds are made up on that one, so just quit your bitching. Sheesh, this guy hasn't changed . . . still bitching!"

"Also," interrupted Helen, "whatever sex the child is, would you be the baby's godfather? It would mean so very much to both of us."

"I truly am honored, my friends. I would really love to do it."

"Good," said Tia. "Now that this burning issue has been settled, let's eat!" She passed out plates and everyone was treated to the splendid, spicy taste of Tia's chicken and freshly made, chilled potato salad. When all had eaten, Tia spoke, and a very serious look appeared on her face. "You know. You *all* have me at a disadvantage here."

"Whatever do you mean, Tia?" asked Helen.

"I've taken care of Tony for many months. He trusts me just about as much as he trusts his mother. We're so close, in mind and spirit, but . . . I still don't really know what it was he did!"

"You mean he *never* told you?" asked Jim.

"Never."

"Forgive me for being so rude, Tia," pleaded Jim. "Tony, you jerk! Why didn't you tell her?"

"I just couldn't talk about it, Jim. Even now, I wake up in cold sweats from nightmares so real . . . it's almost as though I were there again."

"I understand, Tony. But it's very obvious to me this woman has given so much of herself to you. Why . . . I'll never really understand. But I feel she has a right to know."

"Okay, damnit!" snapped Tony. "If she needs to know so bad, then *you* tell her!"

"Never mind!" Tia interrupted. "I don't really need to know

anyway. Just forget it."

"*Yes*, you do," Jim disagreed. "And Tony's going to tell you, or *else*."

"Or else . . . what?"

"Or else, bed-ridden or not, I'm gonna knock your damn face in for being so stubborn!"

"Stop it!" yelled Helen. "If he doesn't want to talk . . . he doesn't have to. That's his right, and *we* should respect it."

"Thank you, ma'am. They only mean well. I guess Jim wants me to get this monkey off my back, and Tia just wants to understand me better. I do owe them that much at least. Please forgive my Italian pride. It sometimes gets between me and my friends. Where shall we start, Jim?"

"Well, Tony, I suppose the beginning is always the safest bet!"

"You don't have to do this, Tony," said Tia with concern.

"I know, honey . . . but I will anyway. So here goes . . . short and sweet!"

Everyone settled back while Tia poured each a fresh glass of beer. They all listened intently, as Tony began the story which carried the weight of a mountain of bricks, burning away at his soul like the fires of eternal damnation.

Chapter 38

Tony stared off into the blackness of the inner sanctum of his tortured mind. Effortlessly, he drew from total recall, the grisly events which led up to this very moment. It seemed to the others, Tony had completely left this time and place, as he returned himself to the horrors of the past. "It was summer, I think," he murmured. "Yes, it *was* summer. The monsoons hammered at us with constant rain most of the time, while Charlie pounded us with rockets whenever he could. The pressure on us was always constant and unbearable. We had to keep our birds flying at all costs, and believe me, those costs were high! Life as I knew it, had changed... for the worst. You could always tell when something died. Even the torrents of clear, clean rain water couldn't hide the smell of death. But you lived with it, and went on, afraid each time you closed your eyes to rest, you might never open them again."

"Jim!" shouted Tia. "Make him stop! This was a bad idea. Please make him stop."

"I *can't* do that, captain," he answered defiantly. "Let him

A Star of Honor

go on. It's something we have to face together . . . we just have to. It's something I just can't explain, but we must do this . . . please." Tia reluctantly agreed, and Tony continued, as sweat began pouring from his forehead.

"I was sitting in the airmans' club getting wasted, when this pal of ours, Will Cutter, was his name, joined me. The music from the jukebox was piercing to the ears, and even here, the smoke burned your eyes. I never really listened to this guy before, but . . . the bottle of scotch he was carrying got my attention. We were both off from work that night, and to get into a little trouble seemed almost inviting! He told me about this Vietnamese chick he was totally spaced out over. He mentioned that she was living in a village about two hours north of here, and needed to get there in the worst way. I figured the guy was either really horny or in love. I found it hard to decide which. I couldn't hear too much more 'cause the music was so loud. Will pointed to the door. We took the booze and departed. When we got outside, he asked me to do him a favor. He said he would pay me boo-koo bucks if I helped him out."

"What did he want with *you*, Tony?" asked Tia.

"Captain, please let him talk!" said Jim loudly. Tony continued to pour out his soul to the only real friends he ever had.

"The favor seemed simple enough. Almost too easy, I guess. I told you before, Tia, I was in this thing to make a quick buck, have fun, and stay one jump ahead of the law. Will asked me to get hold of a jeep we could use for about two days. He knew I had connections with the dudes in the motor pool. Almost everyone on that base owed me something. I told him it would be hard to swing a jeep and a pass, but he kept pestering me. I thought about it for a while, then I told him it would cost five *big* ones for *this* favor. Before the bastard could refuse, he greased my palm with five-hundred bucks . . . *American*. This shit was hard to come by, 'cause we used U.S. government monopoly money called M.P.C. (military payment certificates). I guess they didn't

A Star of Honor

want the enemy to get the greenbacks. What the fuck would it matter anyway? Well, that's beside the point. I took the money and told him to meet me at the motor pool at 0600 hours the next day. I said we'd be bringing two other guys along. He agreed, and we shook on the deal."

"Hell, Tony!" said Jim. "I never knew you had all that money!"

"I asked Jim if he wanted to go on a little trip into the bush for the day. I told him there might be some pussy out there, but he never cared for any of that shit. He was always so much in love with Helen . . . it was disgusting. He decided to go along just for the ride, and we finished the evening playing poker in the back room of the club."

"Yeah, what a big mistake I made that night," mused Jim.

"You bet! Jim never was any good at poker," he grinned.

"I meant going on the trip," he snapped.

"Yes, honey, we understand that," said Helen. "Please continue, Tony," she begged.

"Well, I got the jeep as promised. Will and Jim were waiting patiently at the motor pool. I also got the pass from the security police, so we were ready. We waited in the jeep with the engine running, when I remembered Chuck. He was this black dude we worked with. His name was Charles Poole, but we all just called him Chuck. He finally came running, then joined us. Jim asked me if we were bringing any weapons with us out in the jungle. I told him all I had was my Colt 0.45 I won from the grunt in the poker game, and my good ol' New York switchblade! They were impressed, but I failed to tell them we only had four rounds of ammo. After all, we were lovers . . . *not* fighters! So what the fuck . . . over?"

"*Now* he tells me this," frowned Jim.

"Too late to fuck with it now, buddy," answered Tony.

"All right, guys, take it easy!" ordered Tia. "Let's hold this story right here for now, okay?" We need to get more beer, and I

153

A Star of Honor

really have to go to the potty."

"Okay, mamma-san. You win, baby. You go potty, and bring us back some more beer and chips or something, okay?"

"Okay, good-looking. Can-do-easy! You guys relax and Helen and I will be right back."

The men did as Tia suggested and relaxed, drinking the last drops of remaining beer. They never spoke as they waited, but rather pictured in their minds the gruesome ordeal which would follow.

Chapter 39

Tia and Helen returned with more beer and several large bags of corn chips to snack on, while Tony prepared his mind. "Well, it's about time you got back here, mamma-san!" he remarked. "We sure were getting dry in the throat, baby."

"Oh, Tony, you drink too much beer anyway. You can wait."

"Yes, *ma'am*. Anything you say is fine with me."

"Go on with the story, Tony," said Helen.

"Well, okay, Helen. You talked me into it." They all reclaimed their comfortable positions, as Tia dumped the chips into a large ceramic bowl on the table. Resupplied with beer, the group again became silent as Tony spoke. "We drove on for quite a while, with *yours truly* behind the wheel. Things were going pretty well until we ran out of highway. Will had a map, but said he'd only been to the site once, and wasn't exactly sure if we were going the right way. We turned off the main road and headed down a dirt path leading to the bush."

"I was starting to get a little worried," said Jim. "In addition

A Star of Honor

to us being lost, Tony's driving was scary as hell!"

"Hush, Jim," scolded Helen.

"Sorry, honey."

"Finally," said Tony, "Will recognized the right road to take, and we were soon moving in the proper direction. According to the hand-drawn map, the village was only about twenty kilometers away. Dark clouds loomed overhead, as a storm threatened. I hoped we would arrive before the rains hit, and luckily we did. We heard what sounded like thunder coming from the village. I thought it strange for thunder to only be in that one area, but then, this was a strange place anyway. As we drew nearer to the outskirts of our destination, an ominous mushroom of black smoke was clearly visible. Will was really getting anxious and asked me to go faster. I assured him I had the gas pedal to the floor, and was getting maximum speed out of the jeep."

Tony paused for a moment to sip some beer. He visualized the scene in his mind and went on, transfixed. "Something about that place just didn't look right to me," he continued. "I had this eerie, gut feeling we were about to plunge head first into some mighty heavy bullshit! The closer we got, the more I sensed something really weird about this whole deal. An object was strewn across the road in our path. I drove up to it and stopped."

"What was it?" asked Tia.

"It was the carcass of a dead pig which had been shot full of holes. We all got out and began walking in the dirt past several thatched huts. We found more dead livestock, and then the nightmare began to materialize. A farmer and an old woman lay face down nearby, with their hands tied behind their backs. It seemed to me they had been executed—*mafia-style*. They each had bullet wounds in the back of the head. Before I could ask if the rest of the guys wanted to go on, Will was running into the village. The dead folks up front were a kind of Viet Cong calling card . . . and he knew it. I drew my Colt, and we proceeded on our way. The stench of death, I spoke of earlier, seemed to satu-

A Star of Honor

rate the air. More bodies appeared, some with the heads hacked off. It was really fucked up," he grimaced, clutching the sheets on his bed.

"Stop, Tony!" screamed Tia. "Don't go on, honey. You don't have to!"

"I'm okay, mamma-san . . . really. Now, where was I?"

"You found more bodies," she answered.

"Yes, that's right. The V.C. had already gone, leaving massive destruction behind. Most of the dead were old people, and many women and children. Those beautiful little kids . . . all wasted and for what? I broke down and cried when I witnessed the brutality of it all. Some of the huts were on fire, and everything of any value seemed to have been gone. We spread out to look for Will, and soon we found him. He was sitting on the ground crying, holding a dead woman in his arms . . . cursing. I pried the body from him and tried to make him understand what had happened. It was only then I realized I wasn't too damn sure about what happened myself. I helped him cover the body with a torn poncho, as he explained to me she was his wife of two days, and how he'd planned to desert the service so they could run away together. I called to the others as the storm broke, drenching us with heavy rain. I figured there might be more Viet Cong hiding somewhere close by, so I suggested we get the hell out of there as fast as we could. I was never so scared before, as I was when we ran to the jeep. I scrambled to find the key. Several times I tried to push it into the ignition, but dropped it. The rain was pouring down so hard, we couldn't see two feet in front of us, but we knew we'd have to press on out of there. I finally got the vehicle started, and we took off slipping and sliding, driving as fast as we could across the soggy road. Then . . . the unthinkable happened! We were caught in a crossfire of automatic weapons and our jeep was hit! I gunned the engine, but we rolled over in the mud. As I lay there, I looked around for the others. I crawled like an animal, on my hands and knees, trying to find

A Star of Honor

them. Then I saw Chuck and Will. Each were hit with several rounds across the chest and were killed instantly. As far as I could tell, I wasn't hurt, so I continued searching for Jim. I found him, covered with mud, his stomach ripped open and screaming from the pain. More rounds were fired, but missed—slamming into the tree trunks just above our heads. I hit Jim hard in the jaw to shut him up, so our exact position wouldn't be discovered. I tore off part of my shirt and made a bandage to put around him. All I could see was his blood spilling out, as I twisted the cloth as tight as I could, trying to make it stop. The V.C. left. I thought it might have been because of the storm, but I feared they would return when it was over. We slept that night in the slop and the stink, under the cover of the wrecked jeep."

"Tony, stop now . . . please," pleaded Tia. She shook him briskly, bringing his mind back from the past and quickly returning him to the present. They all quietly pondered his story, while Tia poured another round.

Chapter 40

As they drank the freshley poured beer, all remained spellbound by Tony's breathtaking account. Tia tried to persuade him to stop but he wouldn't budge, determined to continue on with *his* version of the jungle ordeal. When they seemed ready to listen, Tony started again . . . very slowly.

"It was the longest night of my life. The rain seemed to last forever, and I was tired and cold. The jeep offered almost no protection at all, and we hadn't brought any supplies with us. Jim was burning up with fever, and I had no pain-killers or even aspiring to offer him. I'm sure his agony was unbearable, but there was nothing I could do to stop *that* either. As soon as daylight woke us, I tried to figure out a plan to deal with this situation. I wondered how long it would take for the Viet Cong to return to claim their victory prizes from the dead American bodies. I reached the conclusion if we remained we would surely die. I checked the clip in my pistol which was covered with mud. I cleaned it the best I could on my trouser leg, and hoped it would fire . . . if it ever came to that. I survived many times in the streets

A Star of Honor

while growing up in New York. I made it through gang fights and stab wounds in tact, but *this* was different. Now I was on Charlie's turf and *he* had the advantage.

I counted the ammo over and over again. I checked all my pockets to see if I made a mistake. There was *no* mistake, four bullets was all of it, and *that* would have to suffice. I knew we were distinct targets if we stayed there any longer, and decided to make my move while I had the chance. I lifted Jim, carrying him on my back. He screamed from the pain, but soon passed out. I carried him into the bush. I had no idea where I was, but I felt if we continued moving, we had a much better chance. No one was told where we were going when we left, so no one would be looking for us now. Jim and I were down to zero on our options, but we pressed on."

"Did the rain stop?" asked Tia.

"It did stop for a while, long enough for me to see that I was hopelessly lost. I tried to be as quiet as possible, but carrying Jim was no easy task. I had to set him down to rest frequently, and I was starving, losing my strength by the minute. A steak would have been great right about then. I knew dreaming wouldn't get us through this, but leg power might. We traveled slowly all that day. I knew Charlie was out there somewhere, and I felt him watching, waiting for me to fuck up, so he could finish us off!"

"Do you remember any of that, Jim?" asked Tia.

"Some of it, but not all." Tony bandaged my stomach with the sleeves from his shirt, which he had torn off and tied together. I don't remember too much after that."

"I kept pushing myself to move on," interrupted Tony. "I had to keep moving no matter what. I felt those beady little eyes following my every footstep. I never saw any V.C. in the area, until a long, noon-shadow of a person, crossed my path. I got down quickly, covering Jim with grass and leaves so they wouldn't find him if we were caught. Then it happened! Several rounds were fired at me . . . but missed. I dove to the ground trying to hide. I

A Star of Honor

knew Charlie was finished playing now, and he was coming for a piece of my American ass! I drew the 0.45 from my belt, pulled back the slide . . . and prayed. One gook showed himself—standing very close to me. It was my best chance to take at least one of them with me . . . so I took the shot. I hit him in the head. More bullets fired all around me, as a machine gun slashed the tall grass to pieces with each burst. Another Viet Cong made the mistake of crossing my position. Again I fired, dropping him also. I hoped that was the last of them, but my street-wise instincts told me different. I crawled through the bushes, with only two rounds left. I stalked another V.C. who decided this was a good time to take a leak. I aimed, pulled the trigger and . . . my god! I missed! He turned quickly trying to draw his weapon, so I fired my last shot. It hit him in the chest and I watched him fall. I felt now I was in command. I started to bend down so I could lift Jim onto my back. Twigs on the ground, suddenly snapping, caught my attention. I stood frozen in my tracks, as I prepared for the worst."

"What happened after that, good-looking?"

"A loud noise echoed through the jungle, sending monkeys scurrying and a flock of wild birds into frenzied flight. I dropped to my knees, as a piece of hot lead penetrated the flesh of my shoulder. Charlie's Russian made bullet found its mark. Like the stinging of a thousand hornets, it burned its way to the very core of my soul. Another crack followed and I was hit again! I squeezed the trigger of my weapon over and over . . . with no response . . . I fell to the ground. Grabbing onto several vines, I tried to get up, clawing my way to my feet. Still another shot ripped a hole in my body, sending me to my knees. I refused to give way to the pain, as yet a fourth and final bullet struck me. It seemed as though my legs had disappeared, and the whole weight of my body collapsed. Face down I fell, into the mud below. I felt the wrath of Satan in the form of excruciating, anguished suffering. I prayed for God to take me quickly, as my life began to slip away, and the icy fingers of death beckoned me to

A Star of Honor

join her in hell."

    Tears rolled down the cheeks of the Filipino nurse as she hugged Tony, who was now shaking. Jim pulled Helen close to him, squeezing her hand. A peaceful hush settled over the room, as the base flag was lowered outside the window. The haunting notes of a single bugler played taps, to signal the ending of another day.

Chapter 41

After several six-packs of beer were consumed, Tia felt supper should be a priority for the group. She insisted they all go to the hospital cafeteria. After regaining their composure, they followed her advice and went. The mood was still a somber one, as they walked with Tony, who was doing the best he could using the crutches. Few words were offered while eating, as they each reflected in their own way on the awesome account.

Tony insisted on paying for the meal and Tia bought desert. They sat at the table for a while, then decided to go back to Tony's room to hear more details. Although Tia wanted desperately to know what *did* happen she wondered just how good of an idea it really was to go on with that discussion. She realized he was determined, and more than likely would not be deterred from finishing what he started. As they returned to their prior seating arrangements, Tia spoke. "Are you sure you want to go through with this, Tony?"

"Yes, I *do*!" he snapped. "So let's get on with it, okay?" Tia got another supply of beer from the refrigerator and several bags

A Star of Honor

of pretzels. When the beer was poured and everyone seated, Tony continued the story.

"I lay but a few feet from Jim in the mud, believing I was dying. I was face down and couldn't really see where he was, but I had a feeling he was nearby. The Viet Cong that shot me was the last man left of his squad. I assumed he was upset I killed three of his commie friends, but was pleased about the thought of *him* killing *me*! He kicked Jim, and I could hear the thud of a boot crash into the side of his body. There was no response. I feared Jim was already dead. Then, that V.C. kicked *me* in the back. I bit down hard on my tongue, trying not to scream. He rolled me over and kicked me again, but I never moved an eyelash. The little shit was convinced I was dead. I might as well have been, 'cause I couldn't move my legs at all. Charlie figured he had nothing to worry about, and casually built himself a little campfire, making a pot of rice for lunch. I could smell the sewer water he was boiling, and it made me sick to my stomach. When he finished he must have decided to strip the bodies of valuables and press on. He was thoughtful enough to do me first. I think it was because I gave him the most trouble. I reached down ever so slowly, being extremely careful not to draw his attention. Down to my boot I stretched, hoping I hadn't lost my other best friend . . . my switchblade. At first I couldn't find it . . . or my leg. But then, it felt so good to me . . . as I molded my hand around it. I quietly pulled it out, holding it by my side, out of his view. He kicked me again. I suppose this time it was on general principles alone. He got down on his hands and knees, bending over me. He removed my blue sapphire ring from my left finger, and was starting to take off my watch. Now . . . I could have parted with *that* ring . . . no problem! But this fucker was stealing the watch that belonged to my father. It was the only remembrance of dad I had left."

"Did he get the watch, good-looking?"

"Well, almost! But then *almost* doesn't count, except in hand-grenades and horseshoes," he said smiling. "When the

A Star of Honor

gook came closer, I grabbed him by the neck with one hand, pushing the button on the knife with the other. I took full advantage of the element of surprise, and plunged the blade deep into his chest, up to the hilt. He looked into my eyes with a puzzled expression, as I continued to push the knife harder with my last bit of strength. I kept twisting it until I was totally sure the final breath of life was gone from his limp body. He fell dead on top of me. I lay in that position unable to move, for what seemed to me like days . . . the jungle heat wasting no time . . . rotting his stinking corpse. After that, I seemed to lose all track of time. Somehow I managed to push him off, and sighed with relief to be able to breathe again. I was more concerned about Jim, than my own well-being. I heard him groan with pain, as another summer storm dumped buckets on us. The rain was hot. It mixed with the heat of the day and burned my face as each drop struck me. I prayed for God to make it stop, but it kept on pouring. Clawing at the mud, I turned myself over, dragging my way to Jim. He became coherent for awhile and looked at me. He apparently didn't know I was wounded also. He begged me not to let him die there in the bush. I promised him I would never leave him there to die. I hoped I wouldn't die first . . . before keeping that promise. He asked me to get the wallet from his back pocket. I did and handed it to him. Every move was painful for him, as he removed his wedding picture from the pastic holder. He took off his watch and gold wedding band, giving them all to me. He made me promise to take care of them for him . . . just in case. He asked me to make sure his wife, Helen, got them if he didn't make it. I swore to him I would get him out, and he'd be wearing the watch for her again real soon. But . . . I did promise to look out for the stuff in the meantime. He passed out again. As for me, I was going through a combination of numbness in my legs and extreme pain in my back. I dug holes in the mud with my fingers and let them fill with rainwater. I cupped my hands, scooping up the liquid, trying to drink. It soothed my parched throat as it went down. I used a handkerchief from my pocket to gather some of it for Jim. I turned his head to the side, and forced the water down his throat. At first he gagged and coughed, but gradually got used to taking it that way. Food was another problem, but I tried not to panic. I prayed to God for forgiveness of my many sins and asked Him to help me. I promised if He got us through this, I would try to change my life. Then something strange happened. Something I can't explain . . . even now! I think I may have been dreaming, but for one instant, my body felt light as a feather and all my agony was gone. I was bathed in a kind of white radiance, and for that time . . . I was at peace with my soul . . . and my soul was at peace with God. When the feeling subsided, I noticed a snake slithering close to where we lay. I grabbed it quickly, biting off the head. I tore off the skin and ate the meat inside. At first it made me puke, but I knew it was my only chance to replenish my nourishment. I held my nose and swallowed some more. I forced some down Jim's throat whole, and made sure he swallowed it. With my belly full, I slept, but before doing so, I swore out loud that I would survive! I refused to die in that evil, godforsaken place!"

Tony grabbed for his back and fell onto the bed in obvious distress. Tia ran for her black bag and quickly returned with his shot. After his injection, she asked the others leave for awhile to let him rest. Jim and Helen did as they were asked, going out into the lounge area. Tia sat on the bed, holding Tony in her arms. "Rest my baby," she said. "Tomorrow's another day."

Chapter 42

That evening, Jim and Helen were escorted by Tia to downtown Angeles. They bid her good-night as she entered the backseat of a taxi. She handed the driver several silver piso coins to secure her transportation home. Tia was off to her mother's house, while the young couple spent the night at a Filipino hotel. The two Americans enjoyed the following day, exploring together their new and interesting surroundings. Helen was fascinated by the colorful displays of arts and crafts of all descriptions, found in the shops along the narrow, city streets. "The Philippines is a wonderful place! Can we stay here for a while, honey?"

"Sure, baby," replied Jim. "We can stay for as long as you like. You can shop 'till your heart's content. Everything is so inexpensive here, I'm sure it won't murder our budget too badly!"

"Oh, Jim! Stop worrying so much about money. We're on vacation."

"Yes, we are, Helen. But let's not lose sight of the real reason we came here."

"I know, Jim. We came to see Tony. But we can still have a

A Star of Honor

little fun, while we're here. We may never be back this way again."

"You're right, honey. I suppose bad memories . . . die hard. Let's enjoy! I'm sure I won't be coming back this way again . . . *ever*!" Jim took his wife's hand and kissed it. They stopped at a little sidewalk cafe, and ordered several drinks mixed with rum and fruit juice. They enjoyed their short stay in the Philippines as Helen had suggested. In many ways, the experience with Tony brought the couple closer. They tried to prepare their minds for their next meeting with Tony, something they knew was necessary, but would be extremely difficult. They wished to become closer to the airman who saved Jim's life. They wanted so much to help bring him back to reality once again. They realized his road to recovery would be a rough one. Jim and his wife were willing to try whatever it might take to help make it happen, hoping to restore peace and tranquility to their own lives along the way. Later that day, Tia came to the hotel to get them, and they all returned to the hospital where Tony was waiting patiently. They found him sitting in a soft chair reading *The Pacific Stars and Stripes*. "Hi, Tony!" said Jim. "Who's winning the war today?"

"Why, *we* are, of course! I never read this rag, Jim. I just look at the comic strips and do the crossword puzzles. The rest of this crap is all bullshit!"

"You mean you don't think they told us the truth, buddy?"

"Shit, Jim. I don't think they actually lied to us, but rather . . . left out just enough of the important news facts to suit their purpose. We relied on current news too much over there. It's because of that, we never *really* knew what was going on . . . either in Vietnam or at home. I think they at least owed us that much, don't you? Fuck, we fought their war for them, right?"

"I agree, Tony," answered Jim. "It's all been so hard to understand. I really believe the young people of future generations will demand the truth about Vietnam, and this generation will

A Star of Honor

have to give it to them. I feel no malice towards my country for sending us. Back home, they're wounded just like we are. I *know*, I've been there. I've seen and felt what's going on. It's going to take time to heal those wounds . . . they run deep. This damn war's made *everyone* a casualty. Our parents, our wives and girlfriends, our children, and even our future children! They've all been turned into innocent victims, both now and later in their lives, by something as senseless as Nam. It's a kind of total, uncontrollable madness. But I give you my personal guarantee, *they* will demand to know why, and it's guys like *us*, that lived through it, and suffer every day because of it, that will be here to tell them *what* we did over there . . . and perhaps we'll all learn the *why* . . . together." Tony nodded in agreement, squeezing Tia's hand while pouring himself a beer. "I really don't know how you got us out of there, Tony. By using normal rationalization, we should be dead now. You're one tough Italian, that's all I can say. I thank you, and my wife shares that sentiment. And we thank you on behalf of our baby . . . not yet born."

The two men embraced in friendship once again and all remained quiet for several minutes. Tony soon broke the silence, as he continued telling the story. He told of the battles they fought daily against the elements, and reminded them again, about the painful wounds they suffered.

"We ate crawling insects and bugs, as well as that snake! Hell, we even ate weeds and grass, trying to keep up our strength. After what I think amounted to about four days of agony, I pulled myself up to my feet. I had to get us out of there, or we were done for. I don't know how, but I picked Jim up and tried to head south. I carried him until my legs quit on me . . . then I dragged him. I refused to give up my life . . . or Jim's, without a damn good fucking fight!"

"Then you made it to safety on your own?" asked a concerned Tia.

A Star of Honor

"No, not entirely on our own, mamma-san. After existing in the jungle for almost ten days, my body finally gave out, but it was much closer to friendly forces than I thought. Some Army Green Berets, out on a mission . . . found us. The only reason they didn't bag and tag us, was because of an alert sergeant who noticed we were still barely alive and breathing slightly. They carried us to a Marine outpost, dumping us off on *them*. As near as I can figure it, that's when we were split up. The Marines took us to Danang, and we were air evacuated from there to different places. I came here, and Jim went to mainland Japan."

Tia and Helen looked at each other with astonishment. They couldn't completely comprehend what happened, but both agreed the two buddies were lucky to be alive. When Tony was finished he switched on the radio Tia let him borrow. As rock and roll filled the air, he reached for the medals he was awarded by the President. They sat where they were previously discarded, gathering dust on a nearby table. Cupping them between his hands, he said, "I only did what I had to do . . . to survive. Now, don't get me wrong, I love my country and what we stand for as Americans. But, I'm still not convinced I deserve these for what I did. I think others have done more and should have them instead of me."

"Tia opened his hands, removing the medals. She pinned them onto his robe and whispered, "They're yours, baby . . . so wear them proudly, honey. You deserve them, no matter what."

Chapter 43

Tony didn't disturb the medals but still believed someone else deserved them more than he. "I remember the night you came to us, Tony," sighed Tia. "You were a very pathetic sight to behold. At first, I thought your trip to the Philippines might have been in vain. The chart read: multiple gunshot wounds, heavy loss of blood, with acute dehydration. I couldn't even begin to imagine what kind of terrible thing might have left you in such a state. But I saw a strange look of determination and defiance on your face, which told a story all its own. You had a beard, and your skin was deeply tanned and peeled from exposure.

You were clutching an old Army Cold 0.45, covered with mud. When I asked how a patient could be brought in holding a weapon, I was told no one had been able to remove it, all the way from Vietnam to here! It was almost as though the gun had been welded to your palm!"

"I don't remember much about that, Tia. But I do remember seeing *you*, and watching you praying over me like a nun or something."

A Star of Honor

"When patients came to me as bad off as you were, Tony, I prayed for them . . . always. I was told you were given the last rights of the church before you got here. Jacobson decided not to work on you at all. I just didn't see it that way! I pleaded with him to try, but he insisted you were already dead."

"Good ol' Jacobson! I do remember *that*!"

"I told the major you were still breathing," she continued. "But he never wavered from his decision. He pronounced you dead at 0100 hours. I cried, as you were covered with a white sheet. Jacobson seemed so pleased with himself, because he didn't have to expend any excess energy. I felt it was a bad judgment call, and I maintained my conviction you *could* have been saved. Then the strangest thing happened. After treating many patients in the twenty minutes that followed, Samantha thought she detected movement from beneath the sheet *you* were under. I told her she was just tired, and must have imagined it. I knew you were dead, Tony! I checked your vital signs myself!"

"I might have been dead, Tia. That's something only God will ever really know."

Tia continued with her accounting of Tony's arrival, crossing herself at the thought she may have been witness to a miracle.

"Samantha still insisted she saw you move! I was about to scold her again, when I too saw the movement. I ran to your side praying to God Sam was right, and our eyes were not playing tricks. Jacobson was infuriated at the thought of me leaving my assigned station over a dead man. I yanked off the sheet and saw those big, *beautiful* brown, Italian eyes of yours just starring at me. You seemed like a confused infant, just emerging from its mother's womb. You looked as though you wanted to speak to me, trying so hard to force out the words. I *screamed* for the doctor to get his ass over there and I made it crystal clear he screwed up royally! I kept yelling you were alive, but he just ignored me . . . refusing to help. Dr. Williams, an intern, came over quickly to help me. He ordered you prepped and moved immediately

A Star of Honor

into surgery. We all acted fast trying to save you. I put my ear to your lips trying to hear what you were whispering. You asked where your buddy was. You were so worried he didn't make it. I answered your question by telling you your buddy was next to go in for surgery, and I held your hand as you were sedated.

"You mean you lied to me?"

"I don't look at it that way, Tony. I felt if you *were* dying, you should have been able to go in peace . . . with the dignity and respect you deserved. When you were convinced your buddy was safely in our care, you seemed calmer and were able to drift rapidly away, into a deep medicated sleep. I assisted in the O.R., as the surgical team worked for six hours. Several times during the procedure, we nearly lost you, but you fought back like a tiger for every precious second of life, stolen from the grim reaper."

"I do remember some of that, Tia. I felt my body floating weightless, kind of like those guys in space."

"You mean astronauts?"

"Yeah, like that! I must have been dreaming, because I seemed to be drifting towards a bright, glowing presence. Then my father appeared to me. He walked over close to where I was. He looked exactly as I remembered him . . . before he passed away. My dad was a tough guy in life, very hard to get along with. We all loved him very much, in spite of the way he was. I guess he loved me too, even though he never told me so. He pleaded with the presence to spare me, saying his son was too young to be there. Soon after, I found myself back in the hospital . . . waking to the sight of a beautiful Filipino nurse."

"You mean me?"

"Damn right, I mean you, mamma-san!" he snapped. "Yours was the first pretty face I saw when the medication wore off. I really thought I died and went to heaven. I just knew you were an angel, sent by God to care for me."

"Oh, Tony, it was very sweet of you to think something like

that! Perhaps I *was* acting on God's behalf, but actually . . . I was sent by Uncle Sam!"

"Very cute!"

"I thought so too!"

"One thing I never could figure out though."

"What was that?" asked Tia.

"How did the President get the word any of this ever happened, and so fast?"

"I told them, Tony," responded Jim. "I told everyone I could . . . and Helen told everyone else. While I was recovering in the hospital, Helen wrote letters to the Air Force, who must have been too busy with other things to answer. She then wired our congressman, who notified the President. The Air Force researched the incident quickly, but thoroughly, just in time for the President's planned trip to Southeast Asia. I wouldn't be here now . . . if it wasn't for you. So why don't you keep the damn medals! I'm living proof they belong to you! So quit bitching about it, okay?"

"Okay, buddy. You win, and I have something for you, also!" He reached into the tattered canvas bag left in his care, pulling from it Jim's belongings. "Here, buddy. I'm glad you made it . . . I always keep my promises." Everything in the bag was safely returned to Jim, as their eyes once again filled with tears of joy.

Chapter 44

Helen picked up the photograph stained with her husband's blood. She stared at it for a few minutes and began to weep. She truly understood the bonding shared by both men. When she held the picture in her hand, she could almost feel the grief and agony associated with it. At that moment, she expressed her feelings of deepest love, by giving Jim a soft, warm kiss. What she knew in her heart all along was confirmed by Tony's frightening story. Jim was so much in love with *her*, he carried her image in his mind and her name on his lips, even as death stalked him.

Tia saw Tony in a way she hadn't really considered before. Although he was labeled a hero by his peers, it was his compassion for others which had become the most visible to her. She was sure he would deny that . . . as he continued to play the role of a tough-guy. With all the pieces of the puzzle scattered through Tony's head finally coming together, she was able to draw lasting conclusions about him. There was no doubt in her mind, her heart and soul belonged to him, as she realized how deeply in love she had fallen. She prayed silently to God to give

A Star of Honor

her the strength needed to endure this beautiful, newly-found relationship, as she mentally explored the possibilities of Tony being in love with her.

With the many questions about what happened being answered, the small group of friends decided not to dwell on the nightmarish past any more that day. Instead, they made a pact together to arm the world with the truth about the horrible atrocities, of the undeclared war in Vietnam. Their story, only one of thousands, would emerge triumphant, from the deepest ravines of uncertainty, obscured by total desperation, tragedy and death. They wanted everyone to know how the families of U.S. service men and women were literally being torn to shreds, by a war nobody really wanted, and seemed impossible to win.

"I'm going to congress, and then to the American people with this," stated Helen. "I want the politicians to tell me the best way to teach a five year old child his or her father was simply explained away as an *acceptable loss.*"

"You're so right, Helen," said Tia. "But who will listen? The people of the United States are in turmoil. They're so busy trying to deal with their own civil rights, that they just can't be bothered worrying about the broken, mangled, American bodies, littering the filthy rice paddies of Vietnam."

"Easy, girl!" said Tony. "Not *all* the American people think like that. I believe soon they'll all agree on one thing—that this war, no . . . *all* war, is wrong. And maybe some order can be restored to the chaos that's happened there."

"Right on, Tony!" shouted Jim. "I really wouldn't want to get shot again, but however . . . the war was an education for me. I still feel it started for all the right reasons, which got lost in the struggle somewhere. I've seen and felt the wrath of confused America, coming down with a vengeful force, on our brothers and sisters serving their country. I don't believe that *who* started it is important now. *Why* it started is equally as unimportant at this time. What needs to happen now is to bring our people

A Star of Honor

home. America is not used to losing, it looks bad to the rest of the world. So instead, they're trying to turn their backs on the fighting and us, hoping we will all just go away and leave them alone. What I pray for is of course, peace in Vietnam. I want our people remembered as the common folks from all walks of life, called upon by their country to do a job, and who performed that job without due recognition in an extraordinary manner."

"I don't want anything from them people back home," answered Tony. "They know, they fucked up! I don't really care to rub their noses in it just to prove a point. But I agree with one thing though, a little respect *is* in order for us veterans. After all, right or wrong . . . we're all still Americans. We only did what was asked of us, and we shouldn't be chastised for doing it. I admit, my reasons for being there were unique, but that place was responsible for changing my attitude towards other people. I learned about dignity and respect. It was my reason to give up my childhood and begin my long struggle as a man. I also learned of something more precious than anything on God's green earth . . . life. I was never really concerned about it, until I saw death all around me. Death knocked on many doors over there . . . including mine. Color of skin and nationality had no distinction. Little babies were killed right along with fighting soldiers. But I know in my heart, I've become a better person because of the things I was forced to witness and then ultimately be a part of. I also know someday, the slate for us will be wiped clean in the eyes of all Americans. You just wait and see! It will all work out for the best. We just have to hang in there, that's all there is to it! Just a walk in the park. Can you dig it, man?"

"Well, Tony," responded Tia. "You sure have become an optimist about this. Does this mean you now accept recognition for your deeds?"

"I'm sorry, mamma-san, I just can't. As long as I live, I'll never accept *that* as something I really deserve. My mind is made up, so don't even try to make me change it, okay?"

A Star of Honor

"Sorry, baby, but I have my values as well. I won't try to change your mind. I'm sure it will change eventually by itself, when you're able to put the bitterness behind you and finally accept the facts for what they truly are. Tony, whether you want to be or not, you *are* a hero to many people, including me. When we first met, you hurt me every time we talked. I could feel the anger in each word. But now, a change has come over you. It's very becoming, and I love the person you are. But you were always that person, Tony, it just took a war to bring it out. Those qualities were dormant, buried under a duck's ass hairdo and a black leather jacket. You talk of wanting respect from your country, well, baby, it all goes hand in hand. The Silver Star is your country's way of rendering you the proper respect due you, and a simple way to say *thanks* for a job well done. So shut the hell up and pass the *beer*!"

"Oh, Tia, please, no more beer for us," said Helen. "We really must go very soon, and we want to be sober to deal with the traffic between here and the hotel."

"Yes, I think my wife is right, you guys. We better hit the road. We're going back to the states in a few days, and we really could use the rest!" said Jim, winking at Tony.

"Right, Jim, I hear you!" he answered with a typical Tony grin. "I hope you and the Mrs. get plenty of *rest* while you're here in the Philippines. 'Ya know what I mean?"

"Cut the shit, Tony! You're making Helen blush."

"What are your plans now, Tony?" asked Helen.

"Well, I thought I would just take it easy for a while and relax. I haven't mapped out a complete course for myself yet."

"Will you be leaving the Air Force?" asked Jim.

"I don't think so, buddy. The President gave me a waiver to stay on active duty since walking is a part of my life again. But I'll just have to wait and see."

"Well, I guess we really better go now, partner."

"Okay, Jim, that's cool. Tia and I will stop by the hotel to say

A Star of Honor

good-bye to both of you on our way out of town."

"On our way where?"

"What, did I stutter, woman? I said we were going out of town. Do you have any objections, captain?"

"God, Tony, I love it when you take charge like that! Yes, I do have an objection."

"What might that be, mamma-san?"

"Well. A lady would like to be asked first . . . that's all."

"Tia, would you do me the honor of going out of town with me?"

"Of course, Tony. But where will we go?"

"I thought perhaps Baguio or Manila. What do you think?"

"I think we'll discuss this later, okay?"

"Okay, baby. Sorry if I embarrassed you in front of these people."

"*Tony*! I said, later!"

"Well, I guess we need to be going now," said Helen. "I think you two probably need to be alone right now."

Helen gave Tony a hug and Jim shook his hand. They left, promising to return before departing for home. Tia opened a beer and handed it to Tony. After opening one for herself, she said, "What am I going to do with you, Tony?"

"Well, go with the mood, baby. Do whatever you think is best!"

"Right, I think Baguio will do just fine!" She winked at Tony as they kicked off their shoes, relaxing in two soft lounge chairs. "To *us*!" she said, raising her bottle in a toast.

"To *us*!" he responded, and the night drifted lazily by, as sounds of rock and roll continuously filled the room.

Chapter 45

The mellow moment between Tony and Tia was soon rudely interrupted by the opening door. In darted Eric and Samantha, returning from their honeymoon.

"Hi, you two!" shouted Sam. "Have you been sitting here the whole time we've been gone?" she asked, giving a hug to Tia.

"Very funny!" came Tia's reply. "What are you guys doing back so soon?" Anything wrong?"

"No, silly! Nothing's wrong at all! We're just back to get our things together, so we can get an apartment off base until Eric has to ship out." Samantha got close to Tia and whispered something into her ear. It brought a smile to her face.

"See, I told you I was right," said Tia. "You must have been a knockout in that black gown!"

"Well, for as long as it stayed on . . . it was stunning. Even with *me* wearing it!"

"So, Eric, how's married life?"

"Great, Tony. Sam is such a wonderful lady. I really love her!"

A Star of Honor

"Hell, I hope so, pal. You married her!"

"We're trying to get permission from the ol' man to move off base for a while," said Eric. "We ran into a bit of a snag though. It has to clear through Jacobson first before it gets to the hospital commander. It looks pretty bad so far."

"Don't worry about it! I'll handle that jerk! You two will get the permission you need, with or without Jacobson's say so."

"How can you be so sure, Tia?" questioned Sam.

"The hospital commander has been a good friend of my family for many years. He's also a full colonel and a Filipino besides!"

"Now, how did I know she would say that?" remarked Tony, grabbing Tia's hand.

"Did we miss something while we were gone?" asked Sam.

"What do you mean?" said Tia.

"Well, I only meant that you both look like the cat who swallowed the canary, that's all. So tell us what's up!"

"Tony's friend, Jim Garver and his wife, Helen, came to visit from the states."

"Where have I heard that name before?" asked Eric. "Wait a minute! Ain't that the guy Tony was looking to find?"

"That's right. They came for two reasons. First, they wanted to see Tony. And second, they wanted to put both Tony's and Jim's stories together, and arrive at the absolute truth of what happened to them in the jungle."

"And did they accomplish that?" asked Eric.

"Yes, we did!" snapped Tony. "Now, here's a beer! Let's drop the subject, okay?"

"Tony, stop being so rude to Eric," said Tia. "He's only concerned about you, that's all."

"I think we talked about this enough," replied Tony, very annoyed.

Eric looked him in the face and answered, "You're not getting off that easy, pal! We're your friends, Tony. Why can't you

181

A Star of Honor

share a little bit of yourself with us?"

"*No!*" yelled Tony.

"Well, the real truth of the matter is," said Tia. "The man really *is* a hero like everyone's been saying. At the risk of his own life, even after he was wounded, he saved the life of Jim Garver. He also killed four Viet Cong in combat during that action." Eric and Sam just stared in awe at Tony. Since he never discussed what he did at all . . . they were totally surprised.

"Then he really does deserve those medals, huh?" asked Eric.

"You bet he does!"

"Okay, now is everyone satisfied they all know what happened?" asked Tony. "Can we please put this shit to rest now?"

"I knew it all the time, Tony!" said Eric. "I knew you were a hero!"

"Now why would you say that, Eric?"

"Because a true hero would be modest and not want recognition, the way you're refusing it now. Tony, you saved a man's life. That should mean something to you."

"It does, Eric! It really and truly does! That's not what bothers me though. I had to take the lives of four human beings to save that man's life. Somehow it just doesn't add up right."

"Hell, man, it was a war, buddy! People get killed in a war. It was you and Jim or *them*. You made the right decision. You saved your own lives at the expense of four of the enemy, who most likely were guilty of some pretty rotten things . . . but that's not the point. You just did what you had to do to survive. If you wound up being a hero because of that . . . then so be it. You acted by the will of God. If it wasn't supposed to happen . . . it wouldn't have. Their destiny was to die by your hand, and your destiny was to live. I really don't understand how God picks who will live and who will die, but all I know is, after three years of torture, a bomb that killed another . . . set *me* free! I've asked myself over and over since then, why me? Why was I the sole sur-

A Star of Honor

vivor? Why was I the only one able to escape from captivity? You see, Tony? We all have our crosses to bear. I'm sure we'll live with these thoughts for the rest of our lives. But, if the outcome were different, I believe neither of us would be alive at all now. Sure, the faces of my dead crew haunt me every time I close my eyes. But I'm not going to stop living because of that. I have a good woman now, who loves me and understands what I've gone through, and what I'm going through now. I know Tia is just as understanding as Sam. I also know she is in love with you big time!"

"Eric!" snapped Sam. "Don't embarrass Tia like that."

"I'm not embarrassed, Samantha. That's the other thing you missed while you were away."

"What was that, Tia?"

"We figured out all on our own about being in love!"

"Oh, Tia," sighed Samantha. "I hoped that would happen. You two really are a team. Is there anything else you want to tell us?"

"Well, there aren't any wedding bells just yet, so don't get any rumors started, okay?"

"We understand the fraternization regulations that cover relationships between enlisted people and officers," said Eric. "You guys go at your own pace. Enjoy each other and don't worry about the regulations! This is war, and war is hell! Love each other while you can. Life is too short, we never know what lies over the next hill. Your secret is safe with us, and if some day you do decide to get hitched, I'll be glad to dance at your wedding . . . in uniform too!"

"I really appreciate that, Eric," answered Tony. "Are you sure you aren't running for President or something?"

Eric smiled back with an expression that was understood by all. The two men shared a similar destiny . . . they survived and were able to relate to it now. Tia went for more beer as Sam rounded up some drinking glasses. When they returned, Tia han-

A Star of Honor

ded an envelope to Samantha along with a piece of mail that arrived from the United States with Eric's name on it. "These arrived while you were gone," she said. "I'm thirsty, so let's pour some beer before you open them, okay?" Tony poured the beer as Eric and Samantha tore into the envelope like tiny children ripping open Christmas packages.

"Oh my god!" screamed Samantha.

"What is it?" came the reply in unison.

"I got my orders!" she exclaimed, hugging Eric, almost choking him. "I'm being assigned with my husband to Dover, AFB, Delaware! Oh my goodness, there *is* a God!"

"Congratulations, Sam!" said Tony. "I'm very happy for you."

"Yes, I am too," said Tia. "But I'm not happy about training a replacement for you. Damn! I just got you broken in the *right* way too."

The next reaction came from Eric. He stared at the sheet of official looking paper in his hand and seemed as though he were going to cry.

"What it is, honey?"

He handed the typewritten letter to her and she read it to the group. "From the Office of the President of the United States of America. To: 2nd Lieutenant Eric J. Lane. Your outstanding escape, after three years of captivity from a prisoner of war camp in North Vietnam, has been brought to my attention. You are a true and shining example of patriotism at its very best. I am personally inviting you and your wife to the White House upon your return to the United States. At that time, I will decorate you on national television with the Air Force Cross. I have also authorized, effective immediately, your promotion to the grade of captain, as I and your superiors feel you would have achieved this rank during your three year absence. Accounting and finance has worked out all the particulars of the back pay owed you by the government, and a check will be forwarded as soon as possible. What

A Star of Honor

you have given to your country, can never be repaid. God bless you, son. Congratulations on a job well done."

"Damn, Eric," said Tony. "You hit the fucking jackpot!"

"I just don't know what to say."

"Just don't say anything, Eric. We're all so proud of you! Enjoy! You really deserve it!"

Tia left the room and returned carrying a small box. From it she removed a pair of silver captain's bars. "Eric, this was my first set. They brought me good luck, and I want you to have them."

"But, Tia . . . I just couldn't."

"Put a sock in it, pal!" barked Tony. "Oops . . . I mean, *sir*! Let the lady talk."

All remained quiet as Samantha removed the gold lieutenant's bars from his collar and Tia pinned on his new rank. After hugs and handshakes they joined each other in a familiar toast to the occasion. Tony turned up the music as he put his arm around Tia. Eric switched off the lights and a small candle was lit. The silhouette of the newlyweds, pressed tightly together slow dancing cheek to cheek, was softly bathed in the moonlight shining through the window. The magic, mystical scene which ensued . . . would forever remain for each of them, a beautiful romantic memory.

Chapter 46

The two couples partied until after midnight, with all the "cares put behind them and great expectations for their futures weighing heavily on their minds. Eric and Samantha departed for a downtown hotel, wanting to take full advantage of the thirty-six hours still remaining of their leave.

Tony bid his Filipino nurse good-night as she slipped out of the room. He sat down once again in the soft chair pondering the wonderful things that had brightened up his life in the past few days. He realized he might have to go soon, back to the United States to join another aircraft maintenance unit. He was glad he would be able to remain on active duty, but worried about how his horrible nightmares would affect his performance. And then there was Tia. It was her friendship and caring that got him this far, and he would never forget her for it. At that point, he just wasn't sure if he was really in love with her or not. Tony had been afraid of making commitments all of his life, and this time was no exception. *What if I hurt her?* he thought. Over and over in his mind he repeated that line of questioning. He didn't want to ad-

A Star of Honor

versely affect the emotions of another person, but yet, there was that feeling of security and well-being when she was around. In her absence he was lonely, and felt extreme jealousy when other men were near her. He'd never been in love before, but all the tell-tale signs seemed to have materialized.

He liked holding her in his arms and often dreamed of making love to her. He worried about the weekend they had planned together as a result of his idea. When he was totally helpless, things were different. Perhaps he was hiding behind his wheelchair and felt safe from a situation like the one about to happen. He needed this lady by his side, or so he thought. For once in his life he was scared, but for a different reason other than war. The love of a good woman, and possible commitment, was more frightening to him than a New York street fight. He sat up all night weighing all the possibilities. He decided to wait and see. He was sure the weekend would tell both of them exactly what they needed to know. She promised she would come back in the morning. He waited for the familiar scent of her perfume to cross his path. He closed his eyes and pictured her lying next to him, as she did so many times before. He was awakened from his daydream by the softness of her touch gently upon his forehead. "Hi, good-looking, did you miss me?"

"Well, not really. I guess I just had too many other things on my mind."

"I understand, baby. I understand, but I don't believe you."

"Damnit, mamma-san! What do you want from me anyway?"

"Don't get your feathers ruffled. All I want is the truth. That's all I would ever ask of you in our relationship. To tell me the truth no matter how bad the outcome might be."

"You're right, Tia. I guess I screwed up. You seem to know me better than I thought was possible for anyone to know me . . . especially a woman. Yes, I did miss you. As a matter of fact . . . I thought about you all night."

A Star of Honor

"Tony, you stayed up all night thinking of me?"

"Yep!"

"How very sweet of you, but please don't lose anymore sleep over me. I'm not sure I'm worth that much trouble." Tony picked up her hand and kissed it. He rubbed it on his cheek and said, "Tia, you're no trouble at all, and so special nobody could ever estimate your worth."

"Let's stop this. We didn't do this before. We always just kind of let things happen naturally. It seems as though we're becoming two different people, almost as if we are trying too hard to make something happen."

"You're right, baby! Let's just relax and be ourselves, and go for the ride. Whatever will be . . . will be."

"I agree, Tony. Do you feel up to going to Angeles City with me today?"

"Sure! If you don't mind walking slow with a guy on a cane."

"Well, I don't mind if the guy in question treats me to some breakfast!"

"You got a deal, mamma-san! I'll be there in a few minutes. I need to get a shower and a shave."

"Pretty soon you won't need me at all, Tony," she sobbed.

"Why did you say that, honey?"

"Before . . . you depended on me for all those things . . . and now, none of the above."

"Tia, you said yourself, sooner or later the baby bird has to leave the nest. Well, now is the time! But I wouldn't object if you happened to jump into the shower with me on occasion!"

"I guess I'm just being silly, huh?"

"No! It's not silly to care for someone. I couldn't understand that before. But now, after knowing you . . . I've learned so many things. You're such a beautiful lady, with a heart of pure gold. A guy would have to be a fool to let you get away!"

"Well, at least we agree on *one* thing," she smiled, playfully hitting him with a pillow. Tony reached over grabbing Tia

A Star of Honor

around the waist, pulling her down to the bed. He took the pillow from her hands and let it drop to the floor. He kissed her lips softly and said, "Would you object to leaving town a few days early?"

"We can go this evening if you want to. But first we should pick up a few things in town before we go."

"Well, I think tomorrow is better. We need to go say goodbye to Jim and Helen today."

"That's right, I almost forgot. See what your kisses do to my mind!"

"Oh, stop it, Tia! No, on second thought . . . don't stop!" As they resumed their kiss, the door opened and an orderly shouted, *"Room-Ah-ten-hut!"*

Tia and Tony rolled off the bed and landed in a pile of sheets on the floor next to them. They stood at attention as the hospital commander entered the room . . . with Jacobson in tow. "What is the meaning of this, captain?" he shouted. Tia, was for the first time at a complete loss for words. She and Tony looked straight ahead and stood tall as Tia tried to squeeze out a quick excuse.

"Well, sir . . ." she answered.

"No *excuses*! I want you in my office at 0900 hours! Is that clear?"

"Yes, sir!"

"And as for *you*, airman!" he scolded, looking Tony up and down. "I want you in my office when I get through with her! Is that clear?"

"Yes, sir!"

The colonel quickly turned and headed for the door, with Jacobson following close behind. "As you were!" he shouted, as he and the chuckling major left the room. Jacobson stuck his head back inside and said, "I finally got you two right where I want you . . . by the short hairs! Ha! Let's see you fight your way out of this one, hero!"

He then disappeared, leaving the two worried and very sur-

A Star of Honor

prised people, still standing at attention. They were in a state of shock, as they tried to think how to tap dance out of the huge mess that could end both of their careers, with a single stroke of the colonel's pen.

Chapter 47

Tia and Tony sat on a long sofa in the outer office of the command section waiting to be called. Neither said a word as they stared at each other, wondering what the outcome would be. The commander's secretary called for Tia. She swallowed hard, took a deep breath, and stood in front of the big oak door, the only thing standing between her and the *lion's den*. She knocked twice, and was told to enter. She slowly walked up to the desk, and rendered the colonel a brisk salute, as she stopped and stood at attention. "Sir, Capt. Ramos reporting as ordered."

The colonel acknowledged by returning a salute of his own. "Stand at ease, captain. Have a seat." He sat down first, almost sinking into a plush, high-back leather chair, wheeling it to his desk. Tia sat in a smaller chair in front of the desk, which Tony liked to call the *hot-seat*, and now she understood why. She waited for the commander to review the files in front of him. Then he peered over the glasses resting on the bridge of his nose and spoke softly. "Tia, I served with your father in the Korean war. We were the best of friends. I've known you since you were

A Star of Honor

playing with dolls back in your province of Cebu in the southern islands. I know how you were raised and I never expected anything like this from you! You're a sterling performer in the Air Force, with an outstanding record. You're one of my finest nurses in every sense of the word. Now tell me, what the *hell* is going on?"

"Well, sir . . ." she answered.

"Before you speak, captain, I see your troubles began the day this Tony fellow was brought in. I see *all* of our troubles began at that same time! I overlooked the alcohol on the ward, but your people wanted more! Then a party was turned into a drunken brawl, in which you and your nurses participated. A doctor of mine was whacked across the chops with a crutch, and threatened with knives by *your* patient. He was nearly strangled on several occasions! Although I would like to strangle the sonuvabitch myself sometimes. That is conduct unbecoming of a member of the United States Air Force. And now *this*! Fraternization with enlisted folks to the point of making a public spectacle of yourself! I should bust you out of the service and throw him in the barbed-wire hotel for a rock cracking party! "However, I won't do anything until you've had a chance to speak on your own behalf. What do you have to say captain?"

"I'm sure most of the files you have are a bunch of lies reported by that filthy bum, Jacobson. As for my personal conduct, I'm a professional nurse and I always conduct myself that way with my patients. As for the wild party . . . I would do it all again for the morale and well-being of those boys. I saw one of them blow his brains out right on my ward. I will not *ever* let that happen again! As for Airman Magnacavello, I love him and I'm not ashamed of it! If you want to drum me out for being in love with an enlisted man, then colonel . . . you do what you have to do. I don't intend to change this situation for anyone. That's really all I have to say."

The colonel rattled the papers as he thought over the situa-

A Star of Honor

tion. He lit a Filipino cigar he took from a large wooden box, as he pondered what to do. He blew a puff of smoke and tipped his chair back as he began to speak. "Captain, when I listen to you, I can see your father, Raoul. In many ways you are like him. Rumor has it I have been promoted to Brigadier General. Usually these rumors are true. I would hate to see anything happen to that star because of funny business going on between nurses and patients in my hospital. Therefore, nothing like that has happened here that I can see. These reports seem to have come from an obviously overworked doctor on my staff, who must be watching too many movies. You are the finest nurse in this hospital, and to lose you would not be in the best interest of the Air Force. I don't criticize you for who you have fallen in love with for I am in no position to do so. I'm very familiar with what this guy has done, and so is just about everyone on this base! As a senior ranking officer, I cannot advise you to disobey the regulations. But what we don't know, won't hurt us. Be sure of what you're doing. Be sure this love is for all the right reasons. As a man who is speaking off the record now, and who has always been like an uncle to you, my advice is this—if you are so intent on doing this, for heaven's sake keep a low profile. Don't be seen in uniform in public together unless you're conducting official business. Do you understand what I'm saying, young lady?"

"Yes, sir!"

"You are dismissed, captain!" he barked. "Oh . . . wait just one minute, captain. The next time you come before me . . . be in proper uniform!"

"But, sir," she answered, bewildered. "I am in proper uniform!"

"*Major*, don't argue with me!"

"Sir, you called me *major*?"

"Yes, Tia, I did. Congratulations. Your records met the board and you are promoted to the rank of major effective at midnight. Tia stared in disbelief at the commander, who happily puf-

193

A Star of Honor

fed away at his cigar with a great deal of contentment.

"Will there be anything else, sir?"

"No, major. You are dismissed."

Tia stood at attention, snapped a salute, turning quickly towards the door as the commander returned the salute. As she left the room, now filled with cigar smoke, she could hear his voice over the intercom, ask for Airman Magnacavello to be sent in. She winked to Tony as he knocked on the door and waited for his turn in the hot-seat. He opened the door after being told to do so, and stood at attention the best he could, leaning on his cane for support. He saluted and reported in the same way Tia had minutes before. "Be seated, airman!" snapped the colonel.

"Thank you, sir! Ah, excuse me, sir. Can we open a window or something? Smells like something died big time in here!" The colonel was not amused, but said nothing as he read the file on Tony.

"Young man, in the time you have been in my hospital, you have been a major cause of total disruption of the normal operational flow."

"Say again, sir?"

"I said, *airman*, you are a king-size pain in the ass!"

"Oh, I get it now. Thank you, sir."

"That was not a compliment! Are you that stupid or are you putting me on?"

"Sir, I ain't stupid, so don't call me that again. I came here to get my ass kicked, so let's get on with it! You already know what you're going to do, so lay it on me, okay? I just got one thing to say before you do though."

"Which is?"

"Don't blame Capt. Ramos for any of this. I did it all, including grabbing her when you walked in. I guess I got a little stir crazy being in this hospital so long without a female, 'ya know what I mean? She's a fine officer and the best nurse I was ever treated by. She's one of the nicest human beings I know. She

A Star of Honor

worked hard to get where she is, and I don't want to see it fucked up because of me! That's about all I got to say. I guess my ass belongs to you now."

The colonel continued puffing his half-smoked cigar as he read more of Tony's file. He peered over his glasses once again and spoke, "I've never seen an enlisted troop stick up for an officer like that in my entire career! Son, Capt. Ramos explained everything to me already. She can brief you on what was said later. It will only be a warning this time. I feel under the circumstances, no regulations were broken. Off the record, I love that girl like my own daughter. If you hurt her, I will always be around to make your stay in the Air Force miserable. Is that clear?"

"Yes, sir!"

"Be discreet with this relationship because it does not conform with Air Force regulations. Try to stay away from Dr. Jacobson as long as you are here. I am trying to have him court martialed for dereliction of duty. I can't be more specific as to preserve his rights, but your case is one that is top priority on the court agenda. I will assign another doctor to your case while you remain in our care. Listen to Tia . . . as you know, she's good people. And son, last but not least, I have one more thing to discuss with you. I really don't know what has come over Air Force headquarters, but I assume they know what they are doing. These sergeant stripes belong to you, effective immediately!" He handed Tony the stripes and the orders accompanying them as Tony rose to his feet and saluted him.

"Thank you, sir!"

"I guess you have to be a fuck-up to get promoted around here, right sergeant?"

"Oh, I don't know about that, sir! I heard through the grapevine they promoted you!"

"*Dismissed*!" came the very loud order following the remark.

A Star of Honor

"And, sergeant!"

"Yes, sir?"

"You can keep the cigars you thought I didn't see you take from my desk!" he said smiling as he saluted.

Tony returned the salute, scratched his head, and left the room. With a grin on his face from ear to ear, he meandered happily down the hall in search of Tia.

Chapter 48

After searching the hospital halls, Tony finally found Tia in the nurses' lounge. The two held each other tightly, as sighs of relief came from both of them. "Mamma-san, I really don't think I need anymore of this shit!"

"It's okay, Tony. It's over now. Just another bad experience that turned out pretty good in the end."

"Well, major, I understand congratulations are in order!"

"Right, sarge! You think we ought to have a promotion party?" They both looked at each other and laughed, knowing full well how the last party went over with the colonel.

"Well, maybe just a small one," said Tony. "And *no* strippers this time, I promise."

"Okay, Tony. I think a small promotion party *is* in order here. That's been an Air Force tradition for years. The commander shouldn't object to that if we keep it under control."

"Well, Tia, let's just think about it for a while before we make any definite plans. In the meantime, weren't we going downtown to get some things for our trip?"

A Star of Honor

"Right, good-looking. Let's do that now that the fun stuff is over with. Do you want me to get the jeep, or will a taxi be okay?"

"Oh hell, baby, let's just grab a cab. That'll be much quicker anyway. Can we get the cabin again in Baguio?"

"I don't see why not. We can pick up the keys from my mother today when we're in the city."

"Now you're talking, nursie . . . err I mean, major."

"Are you ready, Mr. Smart-ass or what?"

"Okay, Tia, let's go!"

Tony called a base taxi to take them to the main gate. After it arrived, they took it to the checkpoint and exited the car. Tony paid the driver the required amount of money registered on the meter, allowing him to keep the change. Quickly passing the armed gate guards, they entered the street outside the perimeter of the base. Tia waved her hand in the air to summon a Filipino jeepney. She haggled with its occupant over the price of the fare to Angeles City. When she was satisfied the best deal had been made, she and Tony got in. They sped past many shops and other jeepneys in traffic along the way. The aroma of charcoal and outdoor cooking in the streets filled the air. Vendors seemed to be everywhere, trying to sell armloads of every kind of merchandise imaginable. Tony sat close to Tia as she smiled with contentment, laying her head on his shoulder. "This is *not* what I call a low profile!"

"I don't give a shit about what anybody thinks. Let's just do what we want."

"Your attitude is what's always getting us into hot water, do you know that?"

"Sure I do. But you don't expect me to change it, do you?"

"I guess not, Tony. I think nothing could ever change you. That's what I like about you the most. You're not afraid to stick up for what's right!"

"Well, I suppose so, baby. Hey! Isn't that the hotel we

A Star of Honor

should be stopping at?"

"Yes, it is!" she screamed.

Tia excitedly motioned to the driver to stop, tossing him thirty centavos for the ride. He screeched the vehicle to a halt, almost hitting a cart-load of bananas, while scraping the curb. As he sped off honking his horn, Tony and Tia entered the hotel lobby. They checked with the desk clerk for Jim and Helen's room number. After receiving it, they took the elevator to the third floor.

"There it is, room 306. Hope we aren't interrupting anything."

"Oh, Tony. Only you would say something like that!" Tony knocked on the door, and Jim answered.

"Come on in, you two! Have a seat. Helen's taking a shower, she'll be right out. Can I offer you a drink or something?"

"No thanks, Jim," answered Tony. "We just came to wish you a safe journey home, then I'm afraid we need to be going." Helen came from the bathroom wearing a fluffy white bathrobe.

"Goodness! Please excuse the way I look. We got up pretty late today!"

"They stopped by to say sayonara to us, honey. Then they have to hit the road."

"Yeah, we really can't stay long," Tony said. "But it has really been the highlight of my life that you traveled all the way over to the Philippines just to see me. I'm truly honored!"

"It's the very least we could do, Tony," answered Helen. "And it's really us who are honored, by being here with *you*!" Tony hugged Jim and patted him on the back.

"You take care of yourself, buddy. Keep your ammo dry, and take really good care of that lady over there. Keep in touch, huh?"

Jim was almost moved to tears as he returned the warm embrace. "You take care of yourself too, pal. We'll never forget what you did . . . hero!"

199

A Star of Honor

"Aw, shit! Let's not start crying on such a beautiful sunny day in the P.I.!" He leaned over and kissed Helen, while Jim kissed Tia. After the farewells were said, Tony and his lady waved to the couple as the elevator doors snapped shut. Briskly they walked through the lobby hand in hand, strolling out the door as they blended in with the crowd on the noisy city streets of Angeles. They walked to the open market, stopping at a lunch cart for a bite to eat. They drank some San Miguel beer while eating lumpia and rice. Tony stopped an old woman selling flowers, to buy one for Tia. He placed it behind her ear and kissed her softly, as a young boy snapped their picture. He kissed her hand and she helped him to his feet, handing him his cane. They spent several hours shopping and enjoying the sights and sounds of Tia's homeland. Tia then hailed a taxi. As it stopped quickly in their path, they jumped in. It carried them to the home of Tia's mother. Tia introduced the new sergeant to her family, but they already knew who he was because of tall tales previously discussed by Tia's sisters, Lisa and Lett. They reluctantly stayed for supper at the insistence of Tia's mother. After the delicious meal the couple retrieved the key for the mountain cabin and departed for the base. They drove the borrowed red jeep back to save time. They laughed as they headed towards the main gate, brushing rice off the seats and still dragging jungle boots from a previous honeymoon. Tia stopped the jeep just inside the checkpoint, and together they watched the beautiful red sun slowly setting on the horizon, while they held hands tightly, and just simply enjoyed being together and being in love.

Chapter 49

As the sunset disappeared, it was slowly replaced by the eternal blackness of night. Tony suggested instead of waiting until morning, they go to the mountains that evening. Tia wasn't too receptive as she tried to explain the night curfew restrictions placed on traveling in the Philippines. She further explained the increased chances of being preyed upon by bandits operating along the route they were expecting to take. Tony reluctantly agreed to go back to his room and Tia decided to work one more shift so they could get a fresh start the following day. When the next morning arrived, Tia found Tony in bed having a serious nightmare. She left him for a few minutes, knowing that waking him would be nearly impossible. The hospital commander saw Tia as she made her final rounds. He asked her to come to his office, and she did so. "Major Ramos, how have things been working out for you and young Magnacavello?"

"Not too bad, sir. Why do you ask?"

"This came yesterday for the sergeant. Will you see that he gets it?"

"Yes, sir. I will. Might I be so bold as to ask what's in it?"

"Well, officially I can't tell you, major. But if you should happen to see what it is, I don't think it will hurt anything." Tia opened the envelope and read the folded message inside. A sad look came across her face, but she didn't let the news bother her for long. She checked her watch, and hastily returned it.

"I'll see Sgt. Magnacavello gets this, sir. I must be leaving now, as I'm going out of town this morning."

"I assume the sergeant will require a pass to go with you, right?"

"Yes, sir. So very nice of you to offer." The colonel scribbled his signature on the pass and handed it to her.

"Will there be anything else, major?"

"No, sir. Thank you. I'll just be going now, okay?"

"Okay, Tia. Good luck to you both and have fun! Remember, low profile, please!" With nothing more to be said, Tia saluted the colonel and left. She found Tony on the bed in a pool of sweat. He was awake and appeared to be still dazed from his dream. She kissed him and stroked his hair.

"It was another bad one, wasn't it, good-looking?"

"Yeah, it was, honey. But just forget it, okay?"

"Are you almost ready to go to the mountains with me?"

"I was born ready, baby! Just a quick shower and I'll be all set. Say, don't I need a pass to leave?"

"That has all been taken care of, Tony. The colonel was very cooperative today."

"Well, baby, I was packed yesterday, so all we need to do is load the jeep and move out!" Tony took his shower while Tia changed into blue jeans and a green cotton blouse. She put on a pair of white tennis shoes and patiently waited.

"And they say women are slow!" she quipped, as Tony came through the door.

"Quit talking shit, baby. Let's go!"

Tia signed both of them out and they began loading the jeep.

A Star of Honor

Tony begged Tia to let him drive this time. She agreed, but only if it didn't cause him pain. When they were both seated, Tony started the jeep, and they were off to the mountains again, so much in love and so much alone. Tony's hands began to sweat at the thought of going away with a beautiful woman such as Tia, for the weekend. He knew they had progressed far beyond the confines of friendship, but was afraid he would do something stupid to upset everything they worked so hard to find. The jeep bucked and kicked, as Tony tried to manipulate the clutch and shift the gears.

"I thought you knew how to drive this thing."

"I do, baby. But I'm just not used to driving this piece of shit! I prefer the smooth operation of a Corvette Stingray to this garbage can!"

"Well, it doesn't give *me* any trouble, Tony! I think the real reason you got caught when you crashed that night was . . . you just don't know how to drive a vehicle with a stick shift!"

"Very funny, nurse! I can drive anything with wheels on it!"

"Okay, then *drive* and quit grinding the gears!" she snapped. "We do need to get back in this thing you know!"

After Tony finally got the knack of driving the old jeep he took Tia by the hand and smiled. His legs were stiff, but he continued to drive anyway. They went on for several hours, climbing high into the mountains. The city of Baguio lay off in the distance, and both their thoughts drifted back to the first time they were there.

"I never thought I would get to come back here, Tia."

"Well, Tony, I felt like I would be back, but never under these circumstances."

"What circumstances are you talking about?"

"Tony, I get the distinct feeling the rough, tough, street fighter is getting a little bit nervous being alone with a lady, huh?"

"That's a crock and you know it, Tia. I ain't nervous about nothing!"

203

A Star of Honor

"Oh, Tony, please forgive me. I didn't mean to embarrass you. I didn't mean to upset you either."

"Just forget it, Tia. It ain't no sweat, okay?"

"Okay, baby. No problem. Say, don't forget to turn . . . over there on the left."

"Tia, you act like I've never been here before! I know exactly where I am. Turn where now?"

"Back there, Tony. You missed the turn, wise-guy!"

"Aw, shit! Well, I'll just pull a New York u-turn." Tony slammed on the brakes and turned the jeep in the middle of the road, stalling it facing the oncoming traffic.

"Tony, if you wreck us, we're in big trouble! Not to mention we could be killed!"

"Don't panic, baby! I'll get it moving in a New York minute!"

"Well, if you don't," she screamed, "that truck heading this way will make us flatter than pancakes in a Filipino second!" The engine sputtered but started, just in time for Tony to get them out.

"Don't ever do that again!"

"What?!"

"Don't ever show off anymore! It could have gotten both of us killed!" Tears streamed down her face as Tony rolled the jeep to a stop by the side of the road and shut off the engine.

"Okay, mamma-san. What's the *real* problem here? Why are you so damned upset?"

"It's nothing, Tony. I just had a bad night. I shouldn't be taking it out on you. I'm sorry. Let's go on, we need to get things set up at the cabin." He kissed her hand while starting the engine, moving them back out on the highway, this time making the turn. Their arrival at Baguio was soon to follow, as the familiar looking wooden cabin came into view.

"There she is!" yelled Tony. "Just the way we left it! I'll pull up as close as I can to the steps." After Tony stopped the jeep, they got out and stretched their legs. "Give me the key, Tia, and

A Star of Honor

I'll get the door open and get a fire started, okay?"

"Sure, Tony. Do you think you can get a better one started this time, boy scout?"

"Very funny! I fail to see the humor there." Together they pushed the heavy wooden door and Tony carried Tia into the cabin.

"This is very romantic, Tony. I thought a couple had to be married to do something like this!"

"Hell, baby, we don't follow other people's rules! We'll just make our own as we go along."

"Sounds delightful to me, good-looking! Now, when are you going to put me down?" Tia began to get heavy for Tony as his legs began to give out. She hung onto his neck as he went from side to side, and room to room, trying to regain his balance. Tia protested the ride was going a bit too far. Tony tripped over a suitcase and they both fell into one of the big beds in the master bedroom. They hugged each other tightly as they landed in the middle of a soft feather quilt, laughing as they went down. Tony looked at Tia with his penetrating brown eyes, softly kissing her lips.

"Tony," she said, interrupting the kiss. "We need to get unpacked, honey." Tony said nothing as he began to unbutton her blouse. She never moved, as she tried to anticipate what would happen next. Tony stopped what he was doing as he broke into a cold sweat and rolled over onto the other side of the bed.

"I'm sorry, maybe this has been a big mistake."

"No, Tony, not a mistake. We really do have something wonderful here. Don't try so hard, baby. Let's not try to make things happen. I love you, Tony. If it is to be . . . then it will happen on its own."

"I hope I don't disappoint you, Tia. It seems like a million years have passed from the time I got shot until now. I may never get past where we are now."

"Don't worry so much, good-looking. Things will work

A Star of Honor

themselves out. What's bothering you about this?"

"Well, Tia, I never took a friend to bed before and I'm having a little trouble dealing with it."

"Have you ever had a woman for a friend?"

"No, never. Maybe that's my problem, honey."

"Tony, your palms are sweating. Are you afraid of a sweet little Filipino girl, like me?"

"Woman, I ain't scared of nothing!" Tia took his hand and placed it beneath her blouse on one of her breasts.

"See? I'm nothing but flesh and blood. Don't be shy, honey. I'm just a lady who loves you, that's all. I don't bite." Tony removed his hand from her breast, gently pushing back the long black hair from her face with his fingers.

"I love you, Tia."

"I love you too, Tony."

They embraced once more as they both became lost deep in beautiful dreams of love. While they slept in each other's arms, a cool, clean, mountain breeze caressed and soothed their souls, until late afternoon was soon upon them.

Chapter 50

Later that day, Tia was first to be awakened and she tried desperately not to disturb Tony. Gently, she got down from the bed and quietly unpacked their things. She went to the kitchen to begin preparing dinner. She decided to surprise him today with the type of food he loved the most . . . Italian. She wasn't too familiar with how to cook spaghetti sauce, but with the trusty cookbook she purchased, it was worth a try. As she started to saute some garlic in olive oil, the aroma enticed the New Yorker into the kitchen. "What smells so good in here, mamma-san?"

"Oh, Tony, go back to sleep," she pouted. "It was supposed to be a surprise!"

"You're cooking Italian food for me? Baby, that's so nice! Can I help you with something?"

"No thanks, sweetie. I can manage with the cooking myself. Would you like to open the wine?"

"Sure, honey. What kind did you get?"

"Well, I wasn't sure what we should have with this meal, but my new cookbook said red would do splendidly! You'll find it in

A Star of Honor

the icebox. It's Italian wine . . . I picked it out just for us." Tony retrieved the bottle and examined the label. He picked up a corkscrew and started to twist out the cork so the wine could breathe.

"You got Chianti! That's great!"

"Tony, I want everything for us to be perfect this weekend. It's very important."

"Don't tell me! Is this our double promotion party?"

"Call it what you want, good-looking. I just don't ever want you to forget this special time . . . or me."

"You really have made it wonderful, honey. I'll always remember this time together, but how could you even dare to think I would ever forget *you*?"

"Because, men in the military go away and never come back. They sometimes make promises to ladies they don't really mean."

"What are you getting at, Tia?"

"What I meant to say was, don't feel I trapped you into this weekend, Tony."

"Now that's bullshit, Tia. If you'll remember, this whole weekend was my idea."

"Okay, Tony, you win. Let's not waste precious time by fighting with each other. We seem to be acting like an old married couple, huh?"

"I need a walk outside, baby. I have to cool down a little bit. I've got to think about what's happening here. I'm getting really confused."

"Go ahead, good-looking. Take a little walk and I'll finish making supper."

Tony picked up his cane and limped to the door. He went out on the porch and took a deep breath. There was such a beautiful view of the valley below, that for one brief moment, he forgot all about his stubborn pride that seemed to be getting between them once again. After a while, Tia joined him outside.

A Star of Honor

She handed him a glass of red wine.

"I really do love you, Tony." He set both glasses down on the rattan table nearby, and pulled her close to him. He softly kissed her lips and answered, "You're one crazy Filipino, you know that? With all those rich officers out there, and all those good-looking guys . . . you picked *me* to fall in love with. Why?"

"Because, Tony. Underneath that street-punk body, you're a very wonderful man. You're a fighter when you need to be, but on the other hand, you're a kind and caring person. You were my knight in shining armor who rescued me from evil, never fearing for yourself, and you did it all right here in this house. Every passing day you're a pain in the neck and a total smart-ass. You're both outspoken and shy at the same time. You're a man in search of a woman some days . . . and a boy in search of a mother on others. You've captured my heart with your mysterious ways. You're stuck with me, sarge, and that's all there is to it. Maybe I was a little crazy to expose my vulnerability to you, but I have no regrets and I would do it all again . . . if I had to. So what do you have to say about that, Magnacavello?"

"That's a very effective speech, mamma-san. But I really don't deserve a sweet and wonderful lady like you. Say, Tia, do you smell something burning?"

"*My sauce*!" she screamed. Tia ran into the house just in time to salvage supper before it burned completely. Tony followed close behind her.

"Did supper survive, mamma-san?"

"Tony Magnacavello, I pour my heart out to you, and all you're worried about is if supper survived! *Men*! Oh hell, I give up!"

"Tia," he whispered, as he gazed deeply into her eyes. "It was you who wouldn't let *me* give up when I thought long and hard about checking out. Now I'm asking you sincerely, not to give up on me. I love you, baby. I really do. And not only that . . . you're one hell of a broad . . . for an officer! Yer ass ain't too bad

A Star of Honor

either you know."

"Tony, I'm your nurse! When did you start noticing my ass?"

"Mamma-san, I noticed your ass from day one! Come to papa-san, you sweet little brown Filipino baby." Tia put her arms around him and squeezed tight. He picked her up, reaching over to turn off the stove.

"Tony, what are you doing? Put me down! That's an order, sarge!" Tony carried her to the bedroom and kicked the door shut, gently laying her down.

"Looks like supper will be late," he grinned, as he slid onto the soft bed, nestling close to her.

"Why, papa-san, whatever do you mean?"

"Just shut up, okay?"

"You can't talk to me that way, I . . . I . . . mmmmm."

He pressed his lips hard against hers, leaving her speechless. With one hand holding her close, he reached with the other and switched off the light. They undressed quickly, and he covered her majestic, sultry bronze figure, with a pink top sheet. Their bodies became molded together in the passionate heat of burning desire. Their love exploded with the force of a volcano, and soon it softly subsided, as they slowly drifted down the cool, endless, crystal clear streams of ecstasy.

Chapter 51

Tony and Tia remained intertwined in each other's arms throughout the night. As the sunlit mountain peaks illuminated their room, Tia reached over and found Tony gone. She called to him but there came no answer. Then without warning, the bedroom door opened and Tony entered, wearing a borrowed Air Force hospital robe. He was carrying a wicker tray with the breakfast. "Good-morning, mamma-san!"

"Good-morning, Tony," she answered, still half asleep. "What are you up to, sarge?"

"I thought I would bring you breakfast in bed. I'm a pretty good cook, 'ya know."

"On the tray sat a lavender orchid, Tony picked in the early morning mist, to make the breakfast special. Tia sat up in bed, trying to stay covered with the sheet. Tony placed the orchid behind her ear and kissed her softly.

"A beautiful flower, for a beautiful lady," he said, kissing her again.

"Oh, Tony, no one has ever done anything like this for me in

211

my entire life. What did you cook?"

"I made you my house specialty. A cheese omelette and bacon. Would you like coffee or tea, ma'am?"

"Tony, this is so sweet! I think I'll have tea, please."

Tony poured her some oriental tea he had found in one of the kitchen cabinets. It gently steamed from the spout of a blue ceramic flowered teapot, into a matching cup.

"This was my father's favorite blend. How did you know?"

"Well, actually I didn't know. I just found it in the cabinet."

"This makes it even more special, Tony."

"I love you, Tia."

"I love you also, Tony. I feel like I'm living in a dream, and I never want to wake up."

"Then don't wake up, Tia. Let's keep the dream alive forever!"

"Tony, don't speak right now, please."

"Why, honey? Did I do something wrong?"

"No, good-looking. You've done everything right! And that only compounds the problem."

"What problem, Tia?"

"Baby, will you set this tray on the table for me, please?"

"Sure. I guess you're full, huh?" He took the tray and placed it on the table.

"Honey, come lie down next to me," she whispered. She raised the sheet, revealing her naked body to him. He dropped his robe and slid under the covers snuggling close to her.

"What's wrong?"

"I guess it's time for Cinderella to turn her dream back into the reality of being an Air Force nurse again."

"Tia, what is it?" he demanded. She reached over to the night table and opened a drawer. She removed an envelope and handed it to him. "What's this, honey?"

"Just read it, Tony. It was given to me by the colonel before we left to come up here. I was very selfish by not giving it to you

A Star of Honor

sooner. I'm sorry."

Tony tore open the envelope and found an official message addressed to him in care of the hospital from the Secretary of the Air Force. He read it and crumpled it into a ball, throwing it on the floor. "It's my assignment. I'll be going to a hospital in the state of Maryland for more rehabilitation, and then I'll be assigned as a flightline mechanic at Andrews AFB, in Washington D.C. My orders will be waiting on me when I get back from here."

"I know, I already read it. I never told you because I had to know for sure . . . if you really loved me."

"And what did you find out?"

"Oh, Tony," she sighed, tears rolling down her cheeks. "What will become of us?"

"I love you, Tia. I don't want to lose you! I'll come back and . . ." She put her fingers to his lips to prevent him from speaking.

"Remember? No promises, baby. I'll treasure this time we've shared as one of my fondest memories. Everything we did together since you arrived in the Philippines, has enriched our lives. I really do love you, Tony. But I'm afraid *we* . . . were just not meant to be."

"Don't say that, Tia! I don't want to leave you. I won't leave you! You're a nurse. Tell them I'm not ready yet! Tell them, honey!" he pleaded.

"But you *are* ready, Tony. If we're both to survive this . . . I must let you go. If we *are* meant to be . . . God in heaven will bring you back to me. I really believe that. Only time and separation can ever be a true test of our love. So don't make any promises, okay?" They held each other tightly as she wiped the tears from his cheeks. She kissed him, then looked deep into his eyes. "What are you thinking, Tony?"

"I'm ashamed of myself, Tia."

"Why, honey?"

"The men in my family don't cry. I suppose the first wimp is

213

A Star of Honor

in my generation." Tia smiled and kissed him once again, rubbing her face against the warmth of his tears.

"Don't ever be ashamed," she whispered, "to show your true heart and soul to someone you trust. I'm deeply honored that you chose me . . . to be that someone."

"Look at us. Crying like babies. Some people wait a lifetime and never find the beauty and warmth we've found in such a short time together. Let's be thankful for what we've got, and let's cherish and enjoy what little time we have left. And you're right, Tia. Somehow the paths of our destinies crossed, and only the will of God can predict our future now."

"You're a very intelligent man, for a street-wise kind of guy! Thank you, Tony."

"For what, honey?"

"For just being you. The man I fell in love with, and I will never be ashamed to admit that fact. But most of all . . . for being sincere and honest with me. You never lied to me about anything, and I respect you for what you've been through, and for the wonderful person you've become because of it."

"Thank you, baby," he sighed. "Right now . . . I needed to hear that, real bad."

Once again they flowed together in the soft and beautiful warmth of their love. Never knowing what sorrows tomorrow might bring, they decided to enjoy their sweet and wonderful passions.

Chapter 52

Several more sunsets were enjoyed by two people who had fallen deeply in love. They were born on opposite sides of the world, but thrown together as a direct result of the tragedy of a war. They might never have met otherwise and might never have experienced the problems they knew were inevitable and must be faced.

"Have you been thinking of plans for your future, Tony?"

"What's to think about, honey? They're shipping me back to the world. Looks cut and dried to me. I have zero options at this point."

"Tony, I should have left you alone . . . like the many others that passed through my ward, that came before you . . . they simply went their separate ways. I fell in love with *you*, and now we have immense problems."

"Do you really have regrets, Tia?"

"About what, honey?"

"About meeting me, I mean. You know, about being in love with me now."

A Star of Honor

"Tony, the only regret I have is that the lady in question doesn't get to keep the man of her dreams forever."

"But she *can!*"

"How, good-looking?"

"I can get out of the Air Force and come back and marry you."

"Tony, that's a beautiful sentiment, but very unrealistic. I'm afraid when you get back to the United States, among your own kind of people . . . you'll forget all about this Filipino nurse who loves you."

"Tia, how can you say something like that? What do you mean . . . *my own kind of people?*"

"Tony, you know exactly what I'm talking about. A mixed marriage like ours . . . might never be accepted in many communities in the United States."

"That's a cop-out, Tia, and you know it! Why should we give a shit about what other people accept? Hell, we haven't done it up to this point, so why start now?"

"You're right, honey. I am copping out, as you put it. I really just can't come to terms with the fact I'm losing you."

"That doesn't have to be!" he shouted. "We can change that."

"Tony, we once told each other we would mess up a beautiful friendship if we fell in love. I think we were right all along . . . and disregarded our own advice."

"Screw all *that*! I love you, Tia, and you love me! Nothing can change that fact. So marry me, and that will solve everything!"

"Right, Tony. And are you really convinced it *will* solve everything?"

"Yeah. Why won't it?"

"I admit we're hopelessly in love. But at this early stage in our lives, a commitment of marriage made under duress, could hurt us later in life. It could hurt whatever children we may have

A Star of Honor

also."

"I don't believe it, Tia."

"Believe what, good-looking?"

"That you would share with me your heart and soul in one breath, and turn down my proposal of marriage in the next!"

"Tony, love has blinded us. If we married now, it would be a colossal mistake. We're just too young to know if this is really right or wrong."

"That's just fucking great, mamma-san. We're old enough to get our butts shot off in a war, but not old enough to share a marriage? Is that what you're trying to say?"

"Something like that. Tony, are you afraid I might find someone else while you're gone?"

"Hell, Tia, I guess that's your right, isn't it? Would you wait for me . . . if I asked you to?"

"I would wait for you, baby . . . if you asked me to. But please don't."

"What the hell do you want me to do then?"

"Just walk away . . . don't say goodbye, just walk away and don't look back."

"Why not?"

"Because you'll see and hear my heart breaking when you leave. I just couldn't bear that."

"I'll be back for you, Tia." Tia kissed him softly as her eyes began to tear. She held onto him tightly.

"No promises, okay?"

"Okay, honey . . . I understand. I don't like it . . . but I *do* understand."

"Tony, when you leave, I will pray for the winds of time to bring you back to me. If you do come back, that would make it a promise of God. I shall always keep the faith for that day to happen."

"And if it did? Would you marry me then?"

"I might, good-looking. I just might!"

217

A Star of Honor

During their stay at Baguio, Tony was notified by the base he would be shipping out in a few days. They both requested, and were granted, a pass extension by the commander. They spent their remaining time together walking hand in hand through the moonlit, misty mountain nights. They were thankful for the love God had granted them, and for the hours left to share that love with each other in peace. Tony was beholding to this beautiful lady who refused to let him give up on life, and he knew he would never forget her. Tia wondered if this street-punk sergeant would ever come back, and continued privately to believe he would.

As their time together came slowly to a close, they prepared for the trip back to the base. They both knew Tony would leave that day, and their lives would be changed again because of it. As the base was coming into view on the long and dusty highway, Tony squeezed her hand.

"Tony, I won't be taking you to the terminal to watch you go."

"Why not?"

"I want to remember you just like this. I want to cherish this moment in my heart forever." She stopped the jeep at the main gate, but did not enter. Tony unloaded his bags and set them on the ground. Tia took off the gold cross she always wore, and placed it around Tony's neck. "I'll always love you, Tony. Until that someday you return . . . go with God."

Tony couldn't speak, as tears rolled down his cheeks. He looked very professional today, wearing his dress blue uniform. His ribbons were displayed proudly . . . just for Tia. He wore his Purple Heart and above it, the Silver Star. He pulled her to him, never saying a word. They both knew nothing more could be said. They cried and shared so deeply, their final kiss.

Tony picked up his bags and left Tia sitting in the jeep. He showed his I.D. card to the sentry and entered through the gate. He flagged down a taxi to take him to the terminal. As it headed

A Star of Honor

towards the flightline, he broke his word to her. He did look back and saw her waving to him. He watched tearfully, as she faded off into the intricate, winding, twisting, caverns of beauty that would remain enshrined in his memory forever.

Distinguished Service

Upon a wall, the story said,
To Vietnam the young did go.
Some were wounded, some are dead,
While others fates we do not know.

Fear upon a muddy face,
A cold and dreary monsoon rain.
Airlifted from a frightening place,
In blood and bullet-ridden pain.

In hospital beds, the veterans lie,
With solemn hopes, both then and now.
For fallen buddies, all will cry,
In silent prayers, they humbly bow.

As tattered battle flags do wave,
And haunting notes of bugles play.
Bold memories embrace the brave,
Their deeds are now on proud display.

A warmth of soul placed from the start,
For jobs well done, pride overflows.
From bandages hang their Purple Hearts,
As a gentle, golden aura glows.

            Ron Moyne